If She Was To Have Any Man's Child, By Choice, It Would Be Brent's. Which Left Only One Option.

One man.

Could she carry it off? Could she withhold the truth from him long enough to get him to father a child with her?

Amira's stomach churned at the thought of using him. But they'd had a passionate relationship before. Could she hope to stoke that fire of attraction between them again to trick him into impregnating her?

Dear Reader,

Love. Acceptance. Security.

When these have been a constant in your life, too often, you can take them for granted. And that's something that neither Brent Colby nor Amira Forsythe will ever do.

Sometimes I think it's very easy to look at people who "have it all" and to feel envy—even when we're very happy in our world with family and life and work. Amira Forsythe is one of those women it's probably easy to envy. Beautiful, elegant, from a wealthy family—what on earth could she want for?

In *Convenient Marriage, Inconvenient Husband,* Brent and Amira have to overcome the bitterness of their past and forge a new alliance. But how can that be successful when one of them isn't telling the full truth?

I'll leave that to you to find out in coming pages.

With warmest wishes,

Yvonne Lindsay

YVONNE LINDSAY

CONVENIENT MARRIAGE, INCONVENIENT HUSBAND

Published by Silhouette Books
America's Publisher of Contemporary Romance

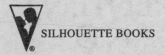

SILHOUETTE BOOKS

ISBN-13: 978-0-373-76923-0
ISBN-10: 0-373-76923-7

Recycling programs for this product may not exist in your area.

CONVENIENT MARRIAGE, INCONVENIENT HUSBAND

Visit Silhouette Books at www.eHarlequin.com

Printed in U.S.A.

Books by Yvonne Lindsay

Silhouette Desire

*The Boss's Christmas Seduction #1758
*The CEO's Contract Bride #1776
*The Tycoon's Hidden Heir #1788
Rosselini's Revenge Affair #1811
Tycoon's Valentine Vendetta #1854
Jealousy & a Jewelled Proposition #1873
Claiming His Runaway Bride #1890
†Convenient Marriage, Inconvenient Husband #1923

*New Zealand Knights
†Rogue Diamonds

YVONNE LINDSAY

New Zealand born to Dutch immigrant parents, Yvonne Lindsay became an avid romance reader at the age of thirteen. Now, married to her "blind date" and with two surprisingly amenable teenagers, she remains a firm believer in the power of romance. Yvonne feels privileged to be able to bring to her readers the stories of her heart. In her spare time, when not writing, she can be found with her nose firmly in a book, reliving the power of love in all walks of life. She can be contacted via her Web site, www.yvonnelindsay.com.

To Bron and to Trish, my wipit buddies.
Thanks for your cheerleading and your constant support.
You guys keep me sane...well, mostly! PTB.

One

"Marry me. I'll make it worth your while."

What the hell was *she* doing here? Amira Forsythe—more frequently known as the Forsythe Princess—was as out of place here in the Ashurst Collegiate Chapel men's room as she was in his life, period. He didn't know which he found more startling. Her demand or the fact she'd actually followed him in here. Brent Colby straightened from the basin and casually reached for a fresh towel. He painstakingly dried his hands and dropped the towel in the deep wicker basket before turning to face her.

His eyes raked over the expensively styled, natural honey-blond hair that tumbled over her shoulders, the immaculate makeup, the exquisitely tailored black suit that hugged her generous curves and threw her luscious creamy skin into sharp relief against its unrelenting somberness. Her fragrance—an intriguing combination of flowers and spice—reached across the sterile atmosphere of the tiled room to infiltrate his senses. Against his better judgment, he inhaled. Stupid mistake, he silently rebuked himself as his blood thickened and heated, pooling low in his groin.

At her throat, her pulse beat rapidly against the single strand of pearls that shimmered in their priceless perfection against the nacre of her skin. A dead giveaway. Beneath that well-groomed exterior, she was scared.

Scared of him? She ought to be. Since she'd left him at the altar eight years ago, he'd had a wealth of anger simmering silently inside. When she'd made it absolutely clear she wouldn't be providing any excuses for her behaviour, he'd rebuilt his world without her in it. For the better.

Brent allowed his gaze to meet and clash with hers, took satisfaction in the way her pupils dilated, almost consuming the icy-blue irises—the distinctively chilling Forsythe stare. Marry her? She had to be kidding.

"No," he replied.

He started to walk past her. Even going back into the chapel where the throng of mourners exchanged platitudes after Professor Woodley's wife's memorial service would be preferable to this. Her hand on his arm halted him in his tracks.

"Please. Brent, I *need* you to marry me."

He stopped and looked pointedly at her ringless

fingers on his arm, not betraying for a second what her touch did to him. How his nerves tautened and his heart rate increased. How he'd like nothing better than to push his fingers through the thick silk of her hair and bend his mouth to the smooth column of her throat. Even after all this time, she still had this effect.

Rather than let go immediately, her grip tightened on his forearm before she eased her hold and contradictorily he wished she hadn't. He didn't know what she had in mind, but one thing, at least, was certain. He didn't want a bar of it.

"Amira, even if I was open to discussion on the matter, this is neither the time nor the place."

"Look, Brent, I know we have some bitterness between us—"

Some bitterness? The woman had left him standing at the front of the church swelled with a couple of hundred guests with little more than a text message to his best man. Yeah, there was "some bitterness" between them, all right. Brent had to fight to hold back the derisive bark of laughter that rose in his throat.

"Please. Won't you hear me out?"

Amira's voice had a tiny wobble in it. Another betrayal of the inimitable Forsythe calm. If her grandmother were alive today, no doubt she'd be deeply disappointed in her only granddaughter, and sole remaining direct descendant, for exhibiting such weakness.

"As I recall, you had your shot at marrying me. You blew it. We have nothing to say to one another." Brent bit the words out through a jaw clenched on all the things he'd like to say. In two long strides he was at the men's room door.

"You're the only man I can trust to do this."

He halted in his tracks, his hand resting on the metal push plate on the door. Trust? That was laughable coming from her.

"I think you'll find you're mistaken. If I were you, I wouldn't trust me not to take you for every last red cent. After all, money is the issue here, isn't it?"

"How…how did you know?"

Brent sighed inwardly before meeting her strained gaze. "Because with your kind it always is."

He should have kept on walking. Engaging in conversation with Amira was the last thing he needed.

"Wait. At least give me an opportunity to explain why. Honestly, I *will* make it worth your while. I promise."

"Like your word is worth anything?"

"I need you."

There was a time he'd have walked through a burning building to hear her say that again, but that time was long past. The Forsythes of this world didn't need anyone. Period. They used people. And when they were done using, they discarded. But there was something in the tone of her voice and the fine lines of strain around her eyes that piqued his interest. That she had a problem on her hands was evident. That she thought he could solve that problem, equally so.

"All right, but not now. I'm working from home tomorrow. Meet me there. Nine thirty."

"Nine thirty? I have—"

"Or not at all." He'd be damned if he'd cater to her social schedule. She'd see him on his turf, on his terms, or not at all.

"Yes, nine thirty's fine."

Amira turned to go. Typical, Brent thought. She got what she thought she wanted. Now he was summarily dismissed. But then she halted in her tracks and turned around.

"Brent?"

"What?"

"Thank you."

Don't thank me yet, Brent added silently. He followed her outside through the chapel and into the adjoining Jubilee Hall of Ashurst Collegiate where, as he watched, she disappeared into the throng. It occurred to him that she must have been the woman his assistant said had been persistently phoning his inner-city office each day and refusing to leave a message when told he was still overseas on business. How on earth had she tracked him down here? He'd only returned late last night in a mad dash attempt to make the service. Attending Mrs. Woodley's memorial was a deeply personal matter, one of respect. It rankled him that Amira had soured what was already a difficult day.

He scanned the hall. He didn't even need to close his eyes to still see the rows of impeccably uniformed boys lined up for assembly each morning, hear the sonorous tones of the headmaster—experience again that sensation of not truly belonging.

He hadn't wanted to come to Ashurst, one of New Zealand's most prestigious private boys' schools, but his uncle, his mother's brother, had insisted, saying even though he didn't bear the Palmer name, he still deserved the education that came with his familial lineage.

That was the trouble with old money. Everyone thought they called the shots, knew what was best for you, if only because it was the way things were "done."

Brent hadn't wanted any handouts. He'd seen what having the Palmers pay his fees had done to his father's pride. Zack Colby might never have had the wealth of his wife's family but he'd taught Brent the benefit of working for his place in the world. As a result Brent had worked his backside off to be awarded one of the rarely bestowed Ashurst Scholarships for Academic Excellence—and he'd repaid every cent to his uncle before he'd left school.

But he hadn't been so perfect a student that there weren't some rough patches. He and his two best friends had excelled at their share of mischief as well. He glanced across the milling crowd of past and present students and faculty members, searching for the faces of his cohorts—his cousin, Adam Palmer, and their friend, Draco Sandrelli. He wasn't disappointed; they were making their way over to him already. Adam was first at his side.

"Hey, cuz. Was that who I thought it was coming out of the men's room a minute ago?"

"What? You need glasses now?" Brent responded with a smile that didn't quite make it to his eyes. He lifted a glass of mineral water from the tray being circulated by one of the waitstaff and took a long quenching gulp.

"Very funny. So what did her highness want?" Adam persisted.

Brent weighed up telling them the truth. There had never been any secrets between them before. Now wasn't the time to start holding back.

"She asked me to marry her."

"You're kidding us, right?" Draco laughed, his faint Italian accent betraying his origins despite the number of years he'd spent living and working around the world.

"I wish I was. Anyway, I'll find out more tomorrow."

"What? You're considering seeing her again? After what she did?" Adam shook his head.

"Yeah. I am. But don't worry. I don't plan on saying yes anytime soon."

Brent looked around the room, scanning for a golden-blond head, but she was nowhere to be seen.

"Do you know why she asked you?" Draco asked, his voice threaded with disbelief and a healthy dose of mistrust.

"Last time I heard from her was that bloody text she sent when we were at the church waiting for her to turn up," Adam added.

Brent clenched his jaw at the memory. They'd been at the altar, the three of them lined up and good-naturedly joking about the lateness of his bride and Brent's soon-to-be married status when Adam's cell phone, nestled in his breast pocket, had discreetly vibrated several times in succession. They'd ignored it. Time had continued to tick past with no sign of Amira. Eventually Adam had checked his phone, his face turning gray at the message.

Tell Brent I can't go through with it. Amira.

Initially Brent had wondered whether it would have made any difference if they'd gotten the message sooner—if he'd been able to get to her house before she'd disappeared with her grandmother—but he'd long discounted that as a waste of energy. And once the shock had diminished into cold, hard anger, he'd cursed himself for a fool for having believed her when she'd said she was different from the mold her grandmother had cast her in.

Back then she'd told him money didn't matter to her, and he'd believed her. In the lead-up to their wedding, though, disaster had struck his business. The container load of imported products, with which he'd swept the young adult games market and seen his fortunes soar, had been faulty. To save Amira from anxiety he'd delayed telling her his first million dollars was slowly being filtered down the drain as he recalled stock and personally backed each and every warranty claim. He'd managed to keep the news quiet for days, but somehow it had broken in the national papers as front page news the morning of their wedding.

It turned out that money mattered to her a whole lot more than she'd admitted. He'd learned that the hard way when she'd sent that text, not even having the guts to face him in person and call things off. Brent always made certain he learned his lessons the first time around. The Forsythe Princess wouldn't get another shot at screwing with his life—or his head—again.

"I have no idea what she's up to, but I'll find out

eventually," Brent replied. "C'mon, let's go and pay our respects to Professor Woodley, then get out of here."

Suddenly all he wanted was the open road and the powerful roar of his Moto Guzzi taking him away from his demons. Together the three men shouldered their way through the throng, oblivious to the admiring glances of many of the women there—young and old—to where a small group spoke with the professor. One by one, the members of the group disappeared, leaving them alone with their favorite tutor from their school days.

"Ah, my rogues. Thank you for coming, boys."

Brent stiffened. He hadn't been called a rogue since the day the professor had caught the three of them demon riding on the dark and winding coast road five miles from school. He could still hear the professor's words of censure when they'd arrived back at their hall of residence, and the disappointment in his voice that they'd taken such crazy risks with their lives.

"All of the students in your year are diamonds... some polished, some still a little rough. All, except you three. You, sirs, are rogues!"

They'd escaped with four weeks of detention and loss of privileges, but none of them had ever lived down the regret that they'd caused the older man such pain with their actions. Especially when they later learned his only son had died on the stretch of road they'd been riding. They'd spent the rest of their final year at Ashurst making it up to him.

"So, how are you all? Married, I hope. There's nothing quite like the love of a good woman, or the constancy of having her at your side." The older man's eyes filmed over. "It's times like this that I realize just how much I'm going to miss her."

"Sir, we're really sorry for your loss." Ever the group spokesman, Adam's voice rang with sincerity.

"As am I, my boy, as am I. But don't think you can dodge me that easily." A faint twinkle appeared in the old man's eyes. "Are you married or not?"

One by one each of them shifted under his penetrating gaze, until he hooted with laughter, drawing the attention of the people around them.

"I take it, not, then. Never mind. I have a good feeling about you boys. It'll happen when the time is right."

"Perhaps marriage isn't for all of us," Brent replied, which only opened up the professor to one of his famous lectures on the sanctity of marriage.

But Brent stopped listening, his attention suddenly caught by Draco's expression. The man looked as if he'd seen a ghost. In the next instant Draco had excused himself and hightailed it across the room, toward the catering staff.

"What was that about?" Adam asked as the professor's attention was taken by another group stopping to give their condolences.

"Don't know, but it looks interesting," Brent answered, his eyes locked on the body language of the tall slender woman with short spiky dark hair, who appeared to be in charge of the catering.

Judging by the stiffness in her pose, she wasn't too pleased to be bailed up by Draco. He smiled at her, turning on the infamous Sandrelli charm; but the woman turned up her nose at him and spun on her heel to stalk away, summarily dismissing him by the looks of things.

"He won't like that," Adam said, and sure enough, after the briefest of hesitations, Draco followed hard on her heels, his face set in a determined mask of intent.

"Looks like he won't be coming on that ride with us after all," Brent noted reluctantly. These days the three of them managed little enough time together. "C'mon. I've had enough of this place. Let's go."

Outside they were treated to the sight of Draco standing in the large circular driveway that opened out at the entrance to Jubilee Hall, clearly trying to persuade the catering manager not to leave. But the woman wasn't having any of it. She put her older model station wagon into gear and spun up a rooster tail of gravel from beneath her tires as she drove away. Draco jogged over to them.

"Don't even ask," he warned, his dark features like a thundercloud as he reached for the helmet on the seat of his bike.

With nothing more than a nod of acknowledgment, Brent and Adam did the same, and before long, the matching high performance bikes were gunning it out of the gates and onto the private road that led to the motorway and back to Auckland City.

From her car, parked beneath the heavy branches of an ancient oak tree, Amira watched as Brent came out of the hall. A tremor shot through her, leaving her hands trembling on the steering wheel of her BMW Z4

Coupe. Damn, just when she'd managed to get her nerves back under control.

The distance between the men's room in the chapel and where she'd parked her car had disappeared into a fugue of disbelief at what she'd actually done. She'd been planning this ever since she'd seen the funeral notice for Professor Woodley's wife. Brent had always spoken so highly of the professor; his respect for the old man was an integral part of him. There was no way he'd miss the funeral. It was the only way she'd be able to see him, to surprise him. She'd visualized how she would meet him, what she would say. She just never believed she'd have either the courage, or the gall, to confront him in the men's room.

Her eyes had eaten up the sight of him. Of the breadth of his shoulders, the green glint in his hazel eyes, the expert cut and fall of his glossy hair that she'd fought not to push back across his forehead the way she always used to.

The past eight years had been kind to him, despite his financial difficulties when they'd parted ways. But then, if the latest New Zealand Rich List was anything to go by, the years had been more than kind. He featured strongly in the top twenty now. She wondered if he still cared about things like that. That kind of recognition had driven him in the past, but there was one thing that had always eluded him—acceptance by the old school, especially when their marriage had not taken place.

Her gaze remained fixed on him as he shrugged into a well-worn leather jacket and pulled his dark helmet on, the darkened visor flipping down to obscure his sharply chiseled features. She'd know him anywhere. The way he moved. The way he held his head.

He was slightly heavier set than he'd been at twenty-five, but it looked good on his frame. There was an aura of strength and power about him that spoke to her on a physical level she hadn't experienced since she'd last been in his presence. Or maybe it was just that. Her own very personal and intimate reaction to his nearness. To his masculinity.

Even now she couldn't believe how she'd managed to pluck up the courage to follow him into the men's room and make her demand. But she'd never before been on the verge of destitution. Need had a way of making you do things that you wouldn't normally do, she thought with a bitter grimace. And she'd do whatever it took to get Brent to agree to her terms.

Amira gripped her fingers around the steering wheel in an attempt to control their shaking. She was going to have to do a whole lot better than this tomorrow if she was going to succeed. She'd crossed the first hurdle; the next stage couldn't be that difficult, could it? She refused to believe otherwise. Brent Colby might be hugely successful but he'd always be the new boy on the block unless he could find favor with the old boys' network that governed the movers and shakers of New Zealand business—favor that had been solidly blocked by her late grandmother at every turn. Now, Amira could give him entrée into that rarefied world. She only hoped he still wanted it as much as he'd once wanted her.

Her future, everything that was important to her, depended on him.

No one could understand how deeply important this was to her. No one. For once in her life she wanted to be taken seriously. To be recognized as having a value to society higher than just being some figurehead or spokesperson—the face behind the people who did all the real work. She could live with the loneliness that engendered—she was used to being put on a pedestal, being isolated. But she could not live with failure. It was too important to her that she succeed this time without her grandmother's influence hanging over her like Damocles' sword.

Isobel Forsythe's death had been the catalyst that had really shaken her up—and not just her death but the draconian terms of the old woman's last will and testament. Amira knew her grandmother had done her best to put a stick in the spokes of this particular dream, but it had only served to make her all the more determined to succeed. Contrary to her grandmother's beliefs, Amira did not hold with the thought that it was unreasonable to promise happiness to those less fortunate. It was her personal mission to see this through. To make something worthwhile of her existence.

She jumped at the roar of the three motorcycles as they swept past where her car was parked. Her eyes inexorably drawn to Brent's form hunched over the powerful bike, taking the lead with the kind of effortless precision with which he approached everything.

He'd been so cold and aloof when she'd tried to talk

to him. Not too surprising given where they were, but he was so distant. Not even betraying so much as a hint of anger for what she'd done to him in the past. And she'd known he was angry—bitterly so. She'd heard of Brent's reaction from her grandmother's solicitor, Gerald Stein, who'd been in the vestibule at the church, awaiting her arrival so he could walk her down the aisle.

Deep inside, her heart gave a painful twist. There'd been no wedding then, but she had to make sure that one went ahead now or her promise to little Casey—and more than a dozen other underprivileged or seriously ill kids—would be broken forever.

He had to agree. He just had to.

Two

Amira hesitated at the gate to the long sweeping driveway she knew led to Brent's home. All she had to do was lower her window and press the button on the intercom; then the gate would be opened. It was all very civilized, so why did she feel as if she was entering a panther's lair?

Clipped hedges lined the sides of the drive toward his riverside property. There were only six houses on this exclusive lane leading to the tidal Tamaki Estuary. He'd really come up in the world. It was a far cry from the inner-city apartment he'd had when he met her.

Time was ticking past and she wouldn't discount him turning her away if she was late. She pressed her window control and reached out to activate the talk button on the intercom.

"It's Amira Forsythe."

Should she say anything else? Did he retain staff at the house, or would he answer the intercom himself?

There was no answer but for the smooth electric hum of the imposing black iron gates gliding apart, admitting her to his private corner of the world. Her hands were slippery on the leather steering wheel as she swept down the driveway.

The front of the house was no less imposing than the gated entrance. Amira pulled her car up in front of a four car garage and made her way toward the entrance of the French Provincial style home. Her practiced eye swept the inviting lines of the house. No expense had been spared on this baby, all the way up to the wooden shingle roof. Her heels clipped over the smooth-honed natural stone pathway leading to the front door.

A shiver of anticipation ricocheted through her as she lifted her hand to the intercom beside the door. Her hand was still in the air as the door suddenly swung open.

Amira's breath caught in her throat at the sight of him. Dressed in Armani, he was a sight to behold. Even her late grandmother couldn't have disapproved of him dressed like this. His dark brown hair was swept back off a wide forehead, not a hair daring to slide out of place today. His shirt remained unbuttoned at the neck, exposing a triangle of warm tanned skin. Had their circumstances been different, she'd be in his arms already. Perhaps even with her lips against that tantalizing triangle, tracing the indent at the base of his throat with her tongue. Her inner muscles clenched on a rising heat that threatened to swamp her.

She forced herself to quell her instinctive reaction to him. To focus on the reason she was here.

"You're on time. Good. Come in."

"I make it a habit to be on time. Especially when it's something as important as this."

Amira stepped over the threshold and into the black-marble-lined foyer.

"Really, Amira? I can remember at least one occasion where you were late. Very late, in fact. But then maybe *that* particular occasion wasn't important to you."

Her cheeks flooded with color. It hadn't taken long for him to refer to their wedding day. It was only to be expected.

"I wanted to explain to you, Brent—afterward. But I knew you wouldn't listen to me."

"You're right. I wouldn't. Which begs the question, why should I listen to you today?"

He stood opposite her—his arms crossed in front of him, his feet shoulder width apart—not inviting her any farther into his home. His body language couldn't be any more defensive than if he'd donned armor and guarded his inner sanctum with a broadsword. One look at the firm set of his sensually chiseled lips reminded her she was not here to fantasize.

"Perhaps I still have something to offer you. Could we—" Amira made a helpless gesture with her hand "—could we sit down?"

"Come up to my office."

Brent spun on a well-polished heel and headed up a wide sweeping staircase leading to the upper level of the house. Opposite the top of the stairs he showed her into a large airy office. The dove-gray carpet muffled their footsteps as they entered the room. Amira looked around—the room was a reflection of the man he'd become since she knew him last.

There was no doubting his success and wealth in the choice of state-of-the-art office equipment, quality furnishings and window treatments—no expense had been spared here, either—but one thing about him, at least, hadn't changed. Built-in glass-fronted bookcases lined the walls. He'd always been an avid reader, and judging by the appearance of many of the book spines, these were not here simply for show.

"You always did love your books," she commented as she perched on the edge of a wing-backed leather chair, her mind suddenly inundated with memories of lying in the sunshine in the park, or at the beach, dozing with her head in his lap, while he read his latest acquisition.

"Among other things less enduring," Brent responded enigmatically as he took his seat behind his desk.

She fought not to flinch as he scored another direct hit. This was going to be more difficult than she'd anticipated. His antipathy toward her filled the air, beating against her as if it had its own life force.

Amira blinked at the light streaming in through the dormer windows behind him. He had her at a distinct disadvantage, purposely she realized. Seated where he was, she couldn't discern his expression or read his eyes like she always used to. She angled her head so she avoided the worst of the morning glare. She'd concede this tactic to him but she'd be damned if she'd concede anymore. Too much rode on the outcome of today, even—as dramatic as it sounded—her very life as she knew it.

"Nice place you have," Amira commented conversationally.

She wasn't about to let him know how nervous she was about this meeting, nor how uncomfortable she felt right now. The contrast between the old memories she'd fought so hard to suppress was at total odds with the distinctly chilly reception she was now subject to.

"Cut to the chase, Amira. We both know this isn't a social visit. What's behind your absurd proposal?"

Amira swallowed and took a deep breath. She had to be honest about it and cut straight to the chase as he demanded. He wouldn't accept anything less.

"Money. As you guessed so astutely yesterday."

Brent laughed, a harsh short sound totally lacking in humor.

"Why doesn't that surprise me? If there's one thing that drives you Forsythes, it's money. At least you're honest about it this time." His tone was scathing.

Amira stiffened in her chair, her back impossibly straight.

"And money doesn't drive you?" she asked pointedly.

"Not anymore," came his succinct reply.

"Somehow I find that difficult to believe."

"Believe what you will. It means nothing to me."

And nor did *she* anymore, she reminded herself. There'd been a time when they meant the world to each other. But that had been torn to pieces on the shattered remnants of their dreams when she'd publicly humiliated him. She couldn't let what she'd done to him that awful day hold her back now. Somehow she had to convince him that marrying could prove beneficial to him too. On the surface of things, she could see that money wasn't a major motivator for him anymore. She had to hope that, on top of the financial benefit she planned to propose, the promise of inclusion into the exclusive old boys' network would be sufficient inducement.

"Fine." She drew in a calming breath. It wouldn't help her cause if she lost her temper now. "As you probably heard, my grandmother passed away recently."

"Yes, go on."

No condolences from him then, she thought bitterly. Mind you, it really was no surprise when her grandmother had barely tolerated him at best—and at worst she'd forced Amira to give him up completely.

"She put certain...conditions on my right to inherit under her will."

"What sort of conditions?" Brent leaned back in his chair.

Although his body appeared totally relaxed, she knew he was alert and listening carefully. Every muscle in that well-toned body was attuned to her, whether he liked it or not. It had always been that way between them. Visceral. Instant. Unquenchable. Even now she felt the electric tingle through her veins that being around him had always brought. It was a distraction she could well do without and one look in his hazel eyes and the remoteness within them forced her back on track.

"Restrictive ones, unfortunately. I must be married before I turn thirty to inherit."

"So you have just under eighteen months to find some poor fool to be your husband." Brent leaned forward on his desk. He flicked his gaze over her body. "With your obvious attributes, that shouldn't be difficult," he concluded dismissively.

"I don't want just some poor fool. I want you." *Oh hell,* that didn't come out right, she thought frantically. An obvious sign of her distress. Normally she was as diplomatic and serene as the media portrayed her.

A small smile played around Brent's lips. "A rich fool like me, perhaps? Sorry to disappoint you but I'm not in the market for marriage to anyone—and certainly not to you."

"No! That's not what I meant at all." Amira hurriedly searched her mind for the words she desperately needed to persuade him to agree to her plan. "Basically, I need a husband. And that's it. I'm not interested in all the accoutrements that come with marriage, or the complications of a relationship. I have more than enough on my plate right now without that. With you, I know I'm safe. There's no one else I can ask who wouldn't expect more from a marriage than what I'm prepared to give. I think I'd be safe to say you have no desire for me anymore so we could agree that it would be purely a business arrangement."

"A business arrangement?"

Finally she'd knocked that reserve from his expression, although she couldn't be sure if what he now exhibited was interest or well concealed mockery.

"Yes, an agreement, between old friends."

His lips firmed into a straight line and he eyed her speculatively.

"And exactly what are you prepared to give to this *old friend?*"

"Ten percent of the value of my inheritance," she named a sum that made Brent's eyebrows raise slightly before she continued, "together with platinum level entry to the Auckland Branch of the New Zealand League of Businessmen."

"All that just for the pleasure of being your husband—on paper?"

There was no doubting the sarcasm in his voice now. Once again color flooded her cheeks.

"I realize you think I'm not exactly a prize, Brent, but even you haven't been able to buy your way into the NZLB. I can ensure that your application is approved. Just think of the contacts it will bring you. I know you have a new project underway in the city and that you've been stonewalled on consents for some time. Delays are costly, especially with the type of waterfront expansion you're planning. A word in the ear of the right people and those problems will disappear.

"I'm sure your lawyer will be happy to draw up some kind of prenuptial agreement that will include the money I'm prepared to give you and the introduction to the NZLB as part of the schedule of what I promise you on marriage."

"What about my money? I assume you want your slice of that too?" His voice remained neutral, as if they weren't talking millions of dollars here.

"Not at all! I don't want a bar of your wealth. That's not what this is all about. You'll be bringing me everything I need by being my husband. You're the one man who can do this for me."

"The only one?"

The way he said it made it like an insult. Amira stood. She refused to be drawn into debate over it. She'd made her pitch. Now the ball was firmly in his court.

"I'll leave you to think my offer over." She delved in her Hermès bag to withdraw a card, which she deposited on the polished mahogany desk. "Here, call me when you've made your decision. I'll see myself out."

Brent watched in silence as Amira left his office. He didn't bother to pick up her card. He knew her number. Had always known it and, try as he might, he'd been unable to scourge it from his memory.

So, she thought she'd be "safe" with him. She had no idea. Safe certainly wasn't the first word that sprang to mind when he saw her. Even the severe gray business-like pinstripe suit she'd worn today did little to hide the tempting shape of her, or the allure of ruffling that touch-me-not aura she projected to the world.

Her belief that he needed her help to gain access to the old boys' network to see him complete his latest development opposite the passenger wharves in downtown Auckland needled him though. He thought she'd have done her homework a little better than that.

Brent Colby needed no one to be a success in his
world. The consents were slow coming through,
granted, but they would come through in the end. It
was all part of the game of showing who held power
in the city, and he was prepared to play that game if
it got him to his goal in the end. Since he'd made and
lost his first million dollars, he'd learned patience—
the hard way. He certainly didn't need Amira
Forsythe's influence.

He should have turned her down flat. Her crazy idea
wasn't even worth thinking over. The fact that she'd
walked away from him when he'd needed her most
should have convinced him of that. That she'd walked
away from him because of money, even more so.

He thought of the figure she'd named as a settlement
if they married. While it was no small sum, it was a drop
in the ocean compared to his current wealth.

But then Amira's grandmother had always coached
her well on the importance of financial security. So
what if she had to shell out a few million to access many
more. He could just imagine what lengths someone like
Amira would go to, to get her hands on his bank balance
now. Even go so far as proposing marriage, perhaps?

And that's where something didn't ring true. Amira
had her own wealth. The Forsythe family were among
the founding fathers of New Zealand, with business
interests that were as far reaching as their reported philanthropy was widespread. And Amira was the end of
the line. The approved line, that was. Brent had heard
rumors of an Australian-based distant cousin who'd

long since worn out his welcome, his credit and his word on the strength of the Forsythe name.

Brent's inner warning system told him there was more to her request than met the eye. Yes, she'd changed in the eight years since he'd last seen her, but she hadn't changed so much that he couldn't tell when she was hiding something from him. And that something piqued his interest.

Brent leaned back in his chair and swiveled it to the window so he could look out over the immaculately manicured lawn leading beyond the tennis court and down to the Tamaki Estuary. He loved this view. The contrast between where he was now and where he'd grown up in a council housing estate across the river was never more prominently displayed than when he looked across the water.

The Amira Forsythes of this world could never understand what it was like to work hard for everything in your life rather than be born into inestimable wealth and privilege by a fluke of nature. He thought back to Amira's grandmother, Isobel. The harridan had barely tolerated him when he and Amira had started going out—and then only because he'd been featured in the nationwide business papers as New Zealand's next up-and-coming entrepreneur.

But that had all changed when the imported products upon which he'd started to build his fledgling empire had turned out to be faulty; and in honoring the warranty requirements, he'd cleaned out every last cent he'd made, and then some. Sure, he could have declared bankruptcy. Reneged on the good faith with which his clients had distributed his stock. But he wasn't that kind of man.

He'd held on to the title to his apartment by the skin of his teeth. With that security he had started the long, soulless road to rebuild his wealth. Bigger than before. Better than before. He knew the value of hard work all right. Over and over again. And that was something that Amira could never understand with her background.

No doubt old Isobel would be turning in the family vault right now if she knew what her precious only granddaughter had proposed. If she'd thought for one minute that her name would be sullied by association with him.

Man, he'd thought he'd struck the jackpot when he'd first met Amira. The Forsythe Princess. With her almost royal demeanor and wealth, and the well-known and much documented disapproval of her grandmother, not many men had dared ask her out. But he had.

Amira hadn't bothered to hide her surprise when he'd approached her at the Ellerslie race track during Auckland Cup Week. She'd been judged overall winner of the fashion parade and had finally extricated herself from the phalanx of photographers when he'd stepped up, tucked her arm in his and led her away from the intrusive glare of flashbulbs. In lieu of a formal introduction, he'd promised her lunch well away from the seething mass of racegoers and the thunder of hooves on the track. To his surprise and delight, she'd accepted.

Their romance had made headlines for weeks as they indulged in the flush of first love. Sometimes dodging the media, others making the most of the publicity to let the world know how lucky they were to be together.

He'd hardly been able to believe his good fortune. He was brash and raw and everything her family wasn't. And yet she'd loved him as passionately as if he were her equal. At least he'd thought she did. But Amira had shown her true Forsythe colors when she'd jilted him hard on the news of his financial failure. Just when he'd needed her support and love the most.

He swallowed against the acidic acrimony of the past. Better he'd discovered it then rather than later, his friends and family had pointed out. But hindsight was no salve to his wounded heart or his tattered pride. She'd hurt him. Cut him far deeper than he wanted to admit—then, or now.

He'd never before considered himself a vengeful man, but as Brent studied the fast-moving flow of the outgoing tide on the estuary it occurred to him that in coming to him Amira had handed him the means to a satisfying stroke of revenge on a gold-edged platter.

His pulse quickened as he thought the matter through. She'd made it clear she didn't want the physical aspects of a relationship, but he doubted she'd resist him forever. Seducing her again would certainly be no hardship. They'd been electric together. Yes, it would give the cutting edge to his plan.

How sweet would it be to stand her up this time, to give her a taste of her own bitter medicine? And how appropriate when she was now the one who stood to lose everything she held dear—the power, the prestige and, most of all, the fortune behind the Forsythe name.

Brent spun his chair back to the desk and reached for his phone, flicking it to speaker and punching in the numbers to Amira's mobile phone.

"This is Amira Forsythe." Her voice filled his office again, and deep inside of him something clenched tight.

"I'll marry you."

"Brent?" she sounded unsure.

"You were expecting it to be someone else?"

"No. I just didn't think you'd make up your mind so soon."

"Afraid you're losing your appeal, Amira?"

"No, not at all. I'm just…surprised, is all, but pleasantly so. Obviously we'll need to meet to sort out a few things. How are you placed tonight? Shall we say dinner at eight thirty?"

She mentioned the name of the waterfront restaurant that had been their favorite haunt so long ago.

"If you're happy to be in the public eye together so soon. It'll raise questions you might not want to answer just yet."

"Rather sooner than later, don't you think?" she replied, totally matter-of-fact. "What time can you pick me up? It's better that we arrive together."

Brent confirmed a time with her that would allow them ample time to get to the restaurant from her place.

"Great. I'll see you then. And Brent? Thank you for doing this. You won't regret it."

The relief in her voice was palpable, making his internal warning system go to high alert and making him even more certain she was hiding more than she was letting on. As he said goodbye and disconnected the call, Brent smiled grimly.

Regret was for fools, and no one had ever accused Brent Colby of being a fool.

Three

Amira let herself into her suite of rooms later that afternoon. She'd managed to finish earlier than expected at the Fulfillment Foundation's office and looked forward to a little down time before going back on show tonight with Brent.

She'd long been thankful she had her own entrance to her rooms at the Forsythe Mansion in Auckland's premier suburb of Remuera. The privacy it gave her had negated the supercilious once-over from her grandmother every time she came and went during the day. It never mattered how immaculate her outfit, how perfect her grooming, Isobel had always managed to convey that she found fault somewhere.

Most people would probably have thumbed their

noses at the matriarch. But Amira wasn't most people. She knew how lucky she was to have been given a home and a future by her grandmother after her parents' untimely deaths in a yachting accident on the Waitemata Harbour. She'd been given every opportunity to get ahead. So, she wasn't the academic genius her grandmother had hoped for, and she took after her mother more in looks than Isobel's own son, Amira's father. But despite her shortcomings, Amira had her strengths and her grandmother hadn't been averse to using them in the course of running the many charities whose boards she sat on. And it had been rewarding work—always. Not least of which because finally there was something Amira was darned good at.

Even now, although she had no need to slip in unnoticed, old habits died hard. She preferred her own small apartment anyway. The sheer size and age of the main part of the house, more like a museum than a home, was overwhelming to most visitors and she'd been no different. Amira had never quite shaken that first impression she'd gained when, after a vicious and public court battle between Isobel and her parents' chosen guardians, she'd arrived to live here. It was more than her bereaved ten-year-old mind could take in.

Isobel had kept an iron grip on all Forsythe affairs up until the last six months before her death, when a series of strokes rendered her incapable of holding the reins any longer. Not a single word had passed the old woman's lips in those last months, but every last glare had been a criticism. For Amira, trying to juggle her grandmother's home care as well as her charity commitments had been wearing in the extreme.

She noticed the message light was flashing on her machine as she kicked off her heels. Amira reached across the table to press the play button. A vaguely familiar male voice oozed from the speaker, making her skin crawl.

"Amira, dar-ling. I've just received the written confirmation of the terms of dear Aunt Izzy's will and couldn't wait to tell you how much I'm looking forward to moving in. Perhaps we can come to an arrangement—a mutually *satisfying* arrangement—about your accommodations. Eighteen months seems so long to wait."

She hit the erase button with a shudder, wishing she could clear the memory from her mind as easily. Roland Douglas, her second cousin on Isobel's side of the family, had about as much presence as a cockroach—and he was just as hard to get rid of. Isobel had long since cut ties from that side of the family, but for some reason, prior to the stroke that had robbed her of her speech, she'd made a codicil to her will naming Roland as default beneficiary should Amira not be married or have "borne live issue" by the time she turned thirty.

Whether Isobel had intended it to be a catalyst, to get Amira to hurry up and find the right kind of man to be her consort as she assumed the Forsythe mantle, no one would ever know. But one thing was certain—without marriage Amira would lose everything, even the annuity that she received to cover her living costs.

When Amira had questioned if her grandmother had

been of sound mind at the time of drawing up the codicil, she'd been assured that a neurologist had sworn an affidavit to the effect that while Isobel was physically impaired her mind remained as sharp as her legendary tongue. She didn't stand a chance of appealing against the will's terms.

Amira stepped through to her bathroom, eager to wash away the taint of Roland's words. He really took sleaze to new heights, and his unsettling phone calls bordered on harassment. If worse came to worse and he inherited, there was no way they'd be coming to any arrangements, satisfying or not.

A shudder ran through her body. Too much rode on her ability to come into her inheritance. Too many hopes and dreams. If marriage was what it took, then marriage it would be.

As she removed her clothes and stepped under the pounding shower, she let the heated water sluice away the tension of the day. Seeing Brent again had been difficult enough, although the stress of that meeting had dissipated somewhat when he'd agreed to marry her. No, the thing that worried her most was the Fulfillment Foundation—the charity she herself had established for the purpose of fulfilling the dreams of sick and dying children and their families. They were running on an absolute shoestring, and her administration staff's wages were now nearly a month overdue.

It said a lot for their belief in her and in the charity that they hadn't up and left by now. But the length of time it was taking to get serious financial backing in a world continually hungry for sponsorship dollars had begun to put the mission of the foundation in jeopardy. Somehow she had to get those wages paid—soon, before her staff were forced to leave and seek other employment.

Going out with Brent tonight was a stroke of brilliance. It would pique public interest in their reunion, and she had every intention of selling their story to the highest bidder. The more conjecture and speculation she could drum up in the short time they had available before announcing their engagement, the better.

Amira closed her eyes and sighed as the shower spray drenched her hair and she lathered up her shampoo. She'd stopped by Auckland's children's hospital, Starship, on her way home from the city and could still see little Casey McLauchlan's face now. All the orphaned five-year-old wanted was the chance to see Disneyland with her new adoptive family. Something that might never happen if her leukemia, now hopefully in remission, came back before the foundation was firmly on its financial feet. Amira had promised the little girl, who'd already lost so much in her short life, she'd have her wish, but the reality of being able to make that happen became more remote by the day.

Brent had said yes, she reminded herself, and if everything went to plan she'd come into her inheritance on the day of the wedding and everything would be all right. She just had to grasp hold of that and make sure it happened.

She'd almost convinced herself of it by the time she'd completed her shower and dressed in a pair of lightweight track pants and a tank top. She had a couple of hours before she had to get ready for dinner with Brent so she might as well make the most of the time, she thought, and indulge in some much missed reading time. She stretched out on her sitting room couch, a towel across the arm of the chair where her hair spread to air dry into lush natural curls, and tried to focus on the words that danced across the page of the novel she'd been trying to read for the past few weeks.

Amira woke with a start to a darkened room and the echo of her doorbell still ringing in her ears. She bolted upright from the couch and took a swift look at the antique carriage clock on the mantelpiece as she stumbled to the door. Damn! It was a quarter past eight already. How on earth had she allowed herself to fall asleep like that?

Brent tapped his foot impatiently as he waited for someone to open up. Just as he reached to press the doorbell again, the door suddenly swung open. His eyes narrowed in appreciation at the sight of Amira, her hair a sexy disheveled mass of curls. One thin shoulder strap of her tank top slid down her arm, and the lack of awareness left by deep sleep remained prominent in her pale blue eyes. As she identified him, the thin fabric of her top peaked around her nipples. She really needed to work on that Forsythe cool.

"Brent! I'm so sorry. I fell asleep. If you can give me ten minutes I'll be ready. Please, come in and pour yourself a drink or something—" She fluttered her hand in the direction of her sitting room. "I'm sure you remember where everything is."

"I'll let the restaurant know we'll be a little delayed."

Brent gave her a pointed look and was amused to see a flush of color steal across the sweep of her cheeks.

"Of course. Look, I'm really sorry about this."

"Don't worry. Just get ready."

Brent silently doubted she'd be finished in the ten minutes she'd said, but she must have moved like the wind because in no time she was back in the sitting room wearing a wraparound gown, in a deep red-wine color, teamed with a set of heels that almost brought her eye to eye with him. She'd tangled her hair up with a bunch of clips on her head, and her makeup, as ever, was immaculate. The Forsythe Princess was very firmly back in residence—a total contrast to the enticing creature who'd met him at the door.

He recognized her shield, for want of a better word, for what it was. He'd identified it early on in their previous relationship. Any time she felt insecure about a situation, she became even more impossibly regal and untouchable than ever. He'd started to gauge how comfortable she was by the height of her heels, and if tonight's ice picks were anything to go by she was battling for supremacy.

"Okay, I'm ready. Let's go," she said, slightly breathless.

"Just one thing."

He might not be able to get her to change her shoes but he could do this. Brent stepped close to her and reached to slide out the pins holding her hair. He let them fall to the floor as he extracted each one then, with both hands, he ran his fingers through the honey-blond tresses.

"There, that's better."

Damn, he shouldn't have touched her. His fingers tingled from the silky contact of her hair, and his body had reacted with a burning awareness that was destined to make their evening very uncomfortable.

Amira gave him an icy glare. "If you say so," she answered before turning a cold shoulder to him and stalking out the door.

Brent held the door of his Porsche 911 open for her, catching a glimpse of her legs as she lowered herself into her seat. He waited a moment, counting slowly to ten, as she scooped up the fabric and arranged it to hide the tempting golden tanned curve of her thighs. He should have brought one of his other cars, something that would have afforded them both some distance between them, rather than this—his latest toy.

As he settled into the driver's seat and fired up the engine, he was too wound up to appreciate the roar of the six-cylinder turbo, and it bothered him that he'd let Amira get under his skin like that. Thankfully the journey from her home on the northern slopes of Remuera to the restaurant on the waterfront was only a short one. Inside of fifteen minutes they were walking along the sidewalk toward the Italian place that had been the scene of so many of their secrets and shared whispers so long ago.

They stepped inside to a bustling and busy atmosphere. The maître d' led them toward the cozily lit table for two in the back corner. Brent rested his hand at the small of Amira's back, smiling slightly to himself as he felt her flinch, then relax, beneath his touch. Well, she'd have to get used to it if she wanted to carry this off. No one would believe an engagement between a couple who never touched.

Heads turned and conversation stopped as they settled at their table, before resuming again more audibly than before. He heard their names being whispered, heard the questions hanging in the air. The rumor mills would be working overtime by morning.

While he was no stranger to the press, he loathed this kind of publicity—being under the microscope for others' entertainment. He'd had enough of that when his first business venture had collapsed, and with Amira's simultaneous abandonment of him it had reached fever pitch. Nowadays he only dealt with the press on his terms and when it would benefit his business.

He was glad that despite the surrounding noise and diners they were afforded some privacy by the partial screening of a large potted palm. As they accepted menus, Brent leaned forward.

"Seems we're already the topic of discussion here. You okay with that?"

Amira looked surprised. "Of course," she replied. "Did you expect I'd cut and run at the first sign of interest? You forget; I'm quite used to it."

Brent shifted back in his seat. Used to it? If anything she looked bored by it. "So it won't bother you that we're going to be the focus of gossip tomorrow."

"It will only be gossip. You know that. I know that. It's all that matters. Besides, when we announce our engagement the forerunning publicity will have been good."

"Good? Why so?"

"Well, we'll be able to get a far higher price for our story if there's been enough speculation about our romance being rekindled, don't you think?"

"Oh, definitely," he said before picking up his menu and studying it carefully.

A cold ball of lead solidified in the pit of Brent's stomach. There it was again. Money. He knew he shouldn't be surprised, but it angered him that her unabashed focus remained the same. For a moment when he'd arrived at her place this evening he'd caught a glimpse of the Amira he'd fallen in love with the first time. The unguarded, private version. But, as she'd just proven with her comment, the real Amira Forsythe sat before him now. The woman who'd greeted him in disarray at her front door was no more real than a chimera.

It wasn't too late to pull out of this charade. He could get up from this table and leave right now. If he did that though, he'd be denied the satisfaction of seeing through his own agenda, and he'd thought about that a lot today. About how he could show her what she'd really said no to when she'd chosen not to fulfill her promise to marry him. By the time she realized what she'd missed out on, he would have his reward. And hopefully, he'd have managed to rid his system of the ghost of her memory for good.

"So when do you think we should make the engagement announcement? Is a week too soon?" She interrupted his thoughts.

"A week?" Brent was surprised she wanted to move this all so quickly. "Don't you think that's a little too soon after your grandmother's death. After all, it's only been what? Six weeks?"

"Hmm." Amira tore a piece off the garlic pizza bread that had been delivered in a basket to their table while they pondered their order. A worried little frown appeared between her brows. "Well, it isn't as if we don't already know one another, is it? A month would be too long so why don't we compromise with a fortnight?"

"A fortnight?" Brent took a sip of the excellent red wine their waiter had poured at his request, then nodded. "Yeah, I think that would be okay."

Amira continued. "And what about the wedding, we're in mid-March now. The soonest I could fit it in would be late May or early June—Queen's birthday weekend probably. Are you free then?"

"Queen's birthday? Yeah, why not?" Since the wedding wasn't going to happen, he really didn't give a toss. He continued. "If you can get it all sorted by then, that'll be fine. I have business commitments after that which would make a wedding impossible before Christmas, and I'm sure you don't want to wait that long to access your inheritance."

While it wasn't strictly true, he saw no reason not to apply his own timeline to her plans.

Amira toyed with the stem of her wineglass, attracting his attention to her long slender fingers, the tips manicured within an inch of perfection. Not so much as a chip of nail polish to mar the facade she presented to the world. He wondered briefly if she'd remain this immaculate when her world fell apart.

"Of course, we won't be able to book anything decent at such short notice." She worried at her lower lip with her teeth before speaking again. "We could always do it at the mansion. There's enough room, and we don't need as many guests as last time. I'll get some publicity people to organize it as soon as possible."

"Publicity people?" This whole situation was crazy enough as it was without turning it into a three-ring circus.

"Well, there's a great deal to juggle between your commitments and mine. I want everything to have the greatest impact." She hesitated and looked at him. "This is a business arrangement after all. We can't leave anything to chance."

"No. We can't."

He shouldn't have been all that surprised, though, he reminded himself. She was brilliant at playing the media. In her token position as glamour spokesperson for the numerous charities her grandmother had favored, she'd perfected her role. It was only to be expected that he, and their wedding, would be given the same polished treatment.

Besides, this time around it was as different from their last wedding plan as chalk was from cheese. They'd made all their plans together—and look at how that had all turned out, he reminded himself ironically.

She was right. It was better to leave this in the hands of a neutral third party.

"How about someone who can handle the organization and publicity releases together? Can you think of anyone who could handle both? The less people involved in this the better. Less room for the truth to come out," he suggested.

"I'll go through a few names I have and compile a short list to discuss with you. We can interview them together if you like. No point in choosing someone you're not at ease with."

"Good of you to realize that," he answered drily. "Are you ready to order?"

"Yes, but there's just one more thing."

"What's that?"

Amira drew in a deep breath before continuing. "How we present ourselves in public. I know I said I wasn't interested in the—" She suddenly looked uncomfortable, a blush coloring her cheeks. "You know. The physical side of things, but I've been thinking it would probably be best if we were to act like any normal couple in love."

Brent reached across the table and uncurled her fisted fingers from where they lay on the tablecloth. His thumb stroked over her knuckles, back and forth. Her eyes flew open and her mouth formed a small O of surprise.

"Like this, you mean?"

She moistened her lips, and he found himself watching the pink tip of her tongue with intense interest.

"Yes, exactly like that," she eventually managed.

He let her hand go and sat up straight. "Sure, no problem. I think I can convince anyone watching that we struggle to keep our hands off one another. How about you?"

"I...I'll manage," Amira said, hiding behind the large menu, effectively ending the conversation before he could provoke her further.

The rest of their evening passed comfortably enough and they coordinated their coming week as to when they could be seen going out together. Amira had a full schedule of engagements for various charity functions, and she'd made it clear she needed him to escort her.

It was as Brent signed for the bill that a bustle of activity drew his attention to the entrance of the restaurant. The maître d' rushed over to him, a worried look on his face.

"I'm sorry, Mr. Colby. I can assure you that none of my staff made the call that brought those people here."

A small, but growing, collection of paparazzi now jostled for position on the pavement, held back by three of the waitstaff from the restaurant.

"Can we use the back entrance?" Brent asked.

"No. Don't worry. We'll go through the front," Amira interrupted before the maître d' could reply. "Perhaps it might be an idea to get someone to bring your car around, though. Save us being hounded all the way to the car park."

There was something in Amira's tone that made Brent assess her carefully after he handed his keys to one of the waitstaff and gave instructions on where his car was parked.

"You don't sound surprised that this is happening."

"I'm not. I made a few calls this afternoon."

"You organized this to happen?"

"Of course. Is that a problem?"

She sat there, as serene as a swan on a smooth lake. The engineer of the bedlam they would be subjected to on leaving the restaurant. He had to hand it to her. She was playing this for all it was worth.

The roar of his car as it was brought to the front, followed by a cacophony of protest from drivers restricted from passing the vehicle where it was double parked on the busy road, drew him to his feet.

"No. Come on, then," he said, determinedly taking Amira's hand in his. "Let's get this over with."

The maître d' walked in front of them, hands raised as if he could ward off the intrusive flash of the cameras and the volley of questions that filled the air. Brent held the passenger door of the Porsche open for Amira and gritted his teeth as she took her time settling into the car. She acted as if she was oblivious to the craziness around them, but he knew she was angling for the best shots as she smiled up at him, the expression on her face luminescent. Finally she was finished, her profile a perfect cameo of disinterest in the paparazzi. Brent strode around to the other side of the car and slid in behind the wheel.

He gunned the engine to a squeal of protest from the tires and pulled out into Tamaki Drive and away from the chaos he loathed. If tonight was a sign of things to come, this was going to be one of the hardest projects he'd ever undertaken. As a fire lit deep in his belly, he acknowledged that there was nothing he liked better than a challenge.

Four

"Did you want to come in for a nightcap?" Amira asked, breaking the strained silence that had stretched out in the car during their journey back to her place.

"Yeah, why not?" Brent agreed, much to her surprise.

He'd been bristling with frustration since they'd left the restaurant. The square line of his jaw tense, his eyes fixed on the road ahead of them—never once making an attempt at conversation.

Inside her suite, she could feel the tension coming off him in waves. She decided to take the bull by the horns.

"You're angry with me," she stated, sliding out of her Jimmy Choos and wiggling her toes in the carpet before crossing to the antique drink cabinet and opening it.

"What makes you say that?" Brent hedged.

"Brent, we might not have spent any time together in the past eight years, but I still know you. You're mad as hell. Why?"

"I don't like being used."

"Used?" She sloshed a measure of his preferred brandy into a handblown balloon and passed it over to him, before dropping a few ice cubes in a tumbler over a Baileys Irish Cream for herself.

"I hate being a public spectacle."

"That was nothing, and you know it. It's the fact it took you by surprise that's made you so mad. So, for that I apologize. In the future I'll keep you in the loop."

"The loop."

Amira hesitated, her glass poised halfway to her lips. There was an undercurrent in his voice that shrieked a warning. She placed the glass down on the coffee table and sank down onto her couch.

"What's wrong?" she asked.

"You make it sound like I'm just a player in this, Amira. A chess piece to be moved around the board at your discretion. We're both in this. We both have something to gain. If you don't include me and if I don't have some input into what is going to happen, you can count on not having my support. I can far more easily withdraw from our agreement than you can."

So there it was: his first threat. Amira thought again of the overdue wages, of the families who needed her help. Of the promise she'd made to Casey. A desperate sigh built up deep inside, a sign of all she couldn't afford to let out, couldn't succumb to. She drew herself up straight, as if she was on an upright high-backed chair rather than the deeply comfortable three-seater designed for sprawling in front of TV.

"I'm well aware of that, and I have apologized. It won't happen again. You know I have too much riding on this to want to jeopardize your commitment."

She allowed herself to relax a little as Brent sat down next to her and took a sip of his brandy.

"To be honest, what you did reminded me a lot of your grandmother. She always did like to be the one pulling the strings."

Amira felt as if she'd been slapped. She lifted her chin in response to the carefully aimed hit. He'd never know how much it had stung. Let him score his point.

"I'll take that as a compliment," she responded.

"Believe me. It wasn't."

He reached over and cupped her chin with one hand, forcing her to look straight into his eyes. She could see the gold rim of color around his pupils and the striations of green and brown that tinted his irises. Her breath hitched as she allowed herself to fall a little into the past—to a time when they'd maintain eye contact across a crowded room as a silent form of communication to express their love. Then suddenly he let her go, breaking the spell that wound about her, reminding her of the gulf that yawned between them.

Reminding her of what she had to do.

If there was one thing she excelled at it was maintaining appearances. She'd never let him know how much he'd rattled her just now. She knew there had been no love lost between Brent and Isobel, and as emotionally cold as her grandmother was she had firmly believed she was acting in Amira's best interests. Besides, despite her enemies, her grandmother had been an incredibly powerful woman.

"Compliment or not, Isobel was highly regarded by the very men you need to get your waterfront project off the ground. Knowing how to pull strings, and which ones to pull, can be a very valuable tool, wouldn't you say?" Amira managed to utter the words with a casualness she was far from feeling.

"Speaking of which, when do you propose to sponsor my admission to the league?"

"I can start tomorrow. Processing can take a while."

"Any chance you can speed it up."

"I'll do what I can. It certainly won't hurt for our new relationship to be in the papers tomorrow. The timing will be perfect. The league is a closed bunch, but they keep their eye on the pulse of what's happening around town."

She might be Isobel Forsythe's granddaughter but she lacked the kudos to make the same kind of demands her grandmother had been famous for—she only hoped that this time they would listen to her. They'd see Brent as an asset to the organization once they looked past his lineage and reputation, she was sure of it. A shiver ran down her spine.

Everything hinged on making this marriage happen— even the roof over her head. The thought was daunting and reminded her of the fine line she had to tread. One misstep and Roland would inherit it all and then she, and her foundation, would be out in the cold. Literally.

Later, after Brent had gone home, Amira let herself into the main part of the house. The air was still, almost as if it was waiting for the mistress of the house to assert her wishes.

Her eyes flicked up to the life-sized oil portrait of Isobel, where it presided over the landing halfway up the staircase. As much as she'd learned to respect her grandmother, theirs had never been a loving relationship. The mere thought that she'd become, or even *could* become, like the old woman was terrifying.

Would she too push everyone away until she died— old and virtually alone? Distanced from those she could have drawn close to her if she'd only shown a modicum of affection? With Amira's current situation she could begin to understand what had driven her grandmother to be the way she was, even if she could never condone it.

Isobel had married into the Forsythe family as a young woman with no more than a nouveau riche background and a fine arts degree to her name. Her union with Dominic Forsythe, the heir to the then-flagging Forsythe fortune, had to all accounts and purposes been a loveless match. Designed more to bolster the coffers of her husband's family and to give Isobel's father acceptance in the marketplace, she had made the best of a bad situation.

It was ironic that Amira was putting herself in a similar position, albeit reversed.

Dominic had swiftly handed over the reins of control

to his new wife when her astute mind and business acumen had proven to be far stronger than his own. Amira wondered if her grandfather had ever felt emasculated by Isobel's strength, or whether their marriage had eventually slid into one of comfortable companionship rather than one embroidered with passion and color. Her own father had been born late into the marriage, when Isobel had been in her mid-forties. He'd been doted on by both his parents, and when Dominic had passed away shortly after his son's birth, Isobel had become even more possessive and controlling than before.

Amira started up the stairs, her hand trailing on the polished wooden balustrade, aware with every step of the cold look of disapproval on her grandmother's features. She passed the landing and continued up the stairs to where her father's portrait was hung.

As a child she'd often slipped out of bed to sit in front of the picture—wondering what her life would have been like if he and her mother hadn't taken their yacht out that fatal stormy winter's day. Her grandmother had, to all intents and purposes, cut her son from her life when he'd eloped with Camille du Toit, the French au pair Isobel had employed to assist the housekeeper at the mansion. Clearly she hadn't wanted to share him with anyone who took his focus away from the fortune she'd amassed, but it had been a harsh shock to her system when he hadn't come to heel when faced with the threat of financial abandonment.

By the time she'd fought the courts for guardianship of Amira, who had been cared for since her parents' deaths by family friends, Isobel had obviously decided she had loved her son too much—given him too much leeway. Amira's upbringing was austere by comparison. Gone was the spontaneous affection she'd been unstintingly shown by her parents. In its place was a disciplined regimen of social and scholastic expectations.

Unfortunately, she hadn't exhibited strong academic tendencies, and it hadn't taken long before it was instilled in her that if she didn't marry well she would never amount to much of anything in her grandmother's eyes. The full weight of trying to earn Isobel's approval had weighed heavily on Amira's teenage shoulders and she'd been massively relieved when she'd shown a forte for the charity work for which Isobel was renowned.

When, about a year ago, she'd pitched her idea for the Fulfillment Foundation to Isobel she'd been crushed to be told she'd receive no support from any of the numerous benefactors that Isobel had on her leash. Besides, Isobel had starkly informed Amira it was creating unreasonable expectations in "people like that."

But Amira remembered what it was like as a child to dream and to wish for things. Things she could never have. And the children she wanted to help had so much less than she'd had in her lifetime. She'd vowed to make the Fulfillment Foundation a success, no matter what her grandmother said. While donations were slowly beginning to trickle in, the foundation still needed operating capital of almost ten million dollars a year.

And so, even in death and with her final flick of the

reins on Amira's life, Isobel had forced her to this—to a marriage of convenience for monetary gain.

Amira looked at the portrait of her father, her eyes swimming with tears.

"It's got to be worth it, Dad. It just has to be."

"Here's the short list of publicity agents who would also be happy to handle event organization for us."

Amira dropped the file onto Brent's desk and sat down in the visitor's chair opposite him. She'd come here this morning to drag a decision out of him come hell or high water. They'd been out numerous times over the past two weeks to a variety of high profile functions, and the number of messages now stacked up on her message service was beginning to make her head ache.

On top of everything, her PA at the foundation had handed in her notice, doubling Amira's workload. It wasn't Caroline's fault. No one could work forever for the sheer love of it. If she'd thought she could have gotten away with it, Amira would have sold off some of the antiques in her suite, but everything was entailed by the Forsythe Trust. She was completely hamstrung.

"Are you sure you wouldn't prefer to handle this on your own?" His voice was a deep rumble from behind the laptop screen, which shielded him from her view.

"Brent, I don't have the time and nor do you. We agreed this had to be done perfectly. It's something we have to delegate."

He swiveled away from the computer and leaned on the desk.

"Fine. Who do you think is best?"

Amira reached over to flip open the file. She spread the photo resumes with one hand; then with her fore-finger she stabbed at one in particular.

"This one. Marie Burbank."

"Why?"

"She has some experience in corporate publicity, but her strength lies in non-profit organizations—which I'm hoping will segue into the charity work I'm in-volved in if we can work well together. Plus, she's worked in event management prior to setting up her own agency."

Brent picked up the resume. "She looks young."

"Which means she wasn't on the circuit last time we were going to get married—she won't be influenced by all the horrid publicity that generated. She's young and she's eager, and because her agency is still new she also has the time to devote to us exclusively. I think that makes her a clear winner, don't you?"

"Bring her on board."

"You don't want to meet with her first?"

"Have you met her?"

"Yes, I thought she came across extremely well. I liked her, and I think we can trust her."

"Good, then if you're ready, let's go."

"Go? Where?" Amira flicked a look at her Rolex. "It's nine now, I have a meeting at eleven in the city. Will that leave us enough time?"

"Depends on how long it takes you to choose."

Brent shut down his computer and tucked it neatly

into its case. Then he shrugged into his suit jacket. He still took her breath away with his dark good looks and impressive build. Her hands itched to reach out and straighten his tie, to flick that tiny speck of lint from his shoulder. Just to touch him for once and know it wasn't staged for other people's benefit.

Amira curled her fingers into a tight fist. She had to stop thinking like that. This was a business arrangement only. There was no room for emotion or need.

For the first time in her life she was grateful for her grandmother's discipline, and she drew on every last ounce of composure as she smoothly rose from her seat and tidied the file back into her slim leather briefcase.

"Choose what?" she asked absently, snapping the case closed.

"Your rings."

"My...? Surely that won't be necessary."

"Everyone is going to expect it. Appearances, Amira. Isn't that what's important? I think Isobel's legal advisers would be pretty suspicious of a wedding with no rings, don't you?"

"Well, what about my old rings. Don't you still have those?"

Brent halted in his tracks. "No. They were among the first things I sold. As you'll remember, I had to liquidate my assets rather quickly at the time."

A surprising pang of loss caught in Amira's chest. Of course he'd sold them. A man like Brent wouldn't hold on to the trappings of the past—especially ones with such a negative connotation. She didn't even know what she'd been thinking when she'd said what she had. She drew in a calming breath.

"Yes, I'm sorry. That was insensitive of me. But really, Brent, I'd prefer not to go ring shopping. After all, it's not as if we're in love or anything. I'll be happy with whatever you choose."

"No. We'll do this together. It might have escaped your notice, but stock in my companies has been steadily climbing since we've started being seen together. I hate to admit it, but you're actually good for me."

He took a step closer to her, close enough that she caught a hint of his cologne. It was still the same one he'd worn all those years ago. The one she'd given him.

"So, what do you say?"

His voice dropped an octave and Amira swallowed. She ached to lean forward just a little more, to press her lips to his and say yes. It shook her to realize, though, that what she wanted to say yes to was more than just his request to choose rings together. She wanted to say yes to him, the man.

Every minute they spent together reminded her, painfully, of what they'd shared before. Of what she'd thrown away. Of what her grandmother had made her do and of how she'd discovered, too late, that she'd been masterfully manipulated into doing exactly what Isobel had wanted all along. All at the expense of her and Brent's happiness. And she'd been foolish enough, naive enough, to let it happen.

"Amira?" Brent prompted.

"Okay. Let's get it over with. I really don't have much time."

Thankfully, he stepped away and gestured to the door. As Amira preceded him down the stairs she began to wonder what toll this was going to take on her. This forced ambivalence to their proximity.

From the dark days after her parents had died she'd craved a sense of true belonging—of being loved and wanted just for herself. She'd had that fleetingly with Brent, but she'd thrown it away. She had believed she'd inured herself to that need. Learned to cope without it. Being with Brent like this just proved the opposite. She needed love, needed him, more than ever before, and it was killing her inside to realize she would never again have his heart.

Five

Brent flicked a glance in his rearview mirror. Amira still followed behind in that cute little BMW of hers. Her reaction back at the house had taken him off balance. He'd have expected her to jump at the chance of a new piece of bling. Okay, well not bling exactly. Something tasteful and understated—and outrageously expensive. Just like her.

He thought about what she'd said—about her old rings. Had she really expected him to hold on to them? He shook his head slightly. As if. He pretty much couldn't wait to rid himself of everything he'd ever associated with her, although holding on to his apartment—the place he'd become her first lover—had been out of necessity rather than for sentimental reasons.

The rent he'd gathered from leasing it had helped him repay his final creditors, and its eventual sale five years later had put him another few rungs back up his ladder. Now here he was. Successful. Strong. Financially secure no matter what might happen in the future.

He wondered briefly, whether they'd have made it—him and Amira—if they'd gone ahead with the wedding. If her highness would have been able to tolerate the cheap and close conditions of the tiny apartment he'd rented after leasing his apartment. If she could have stood the endless tins of baked beans on toast instead of four-star luxury dining, while he made certain every last penny of his debt was repaid.

He flicked another glance in the rearview mirror. It was doubtful. Oh sure, she probably would've given it a shot. Until the first time a cockroach crawled across the bench of the poky kitchenette. She'd have been "her not-so-serene-highness" then.

Anyway, all this conjecture was irrelevant. What was important now was that he carry this thing through to its bitter end. And it would be bitter. Bittersweet for him, at least. It hadn't been easy to forget the effect she'd had on him all that time ago and was even less easy to forget the devastating blow her rejection of his love had wreaked upon him. God, he could still remember that awful cold mummified feeling that had encased his body as Adam had shown him the text message on his phone. Somehow he'd managed to enunciate the announcement that there would be no wedding that day. Hell, he could still count every step he'd taken to the front door of the church, to where she wasn't waiting to walk down the aisle.

From there it was all a bit of a blur. Draco and Adam had caught up with him on the pavement as he stepped forward to hail a taxi, instead turning him around and shepherding him to the car Adam had brought them in to the church. People had begun to spill down the front steps by that stage. Bewilderment painted on many faces. Even the magazine reporters and photographers had milled about in confusion, their attempts to get the first pictures of the happy couple suddenly thwarted.

She'd stood him up with a bloody text message. He still couldn't believe it. He'd made Adam drive him to the Forsythe mansion where the housekeeper very coolly informed him that Mrs. and Miss Forsythe were both not at home and were not expected back for some time. He'd returned to his apartment at that point— certain he never wanted to see or hear from her again.

It had been a disastrous end to the week from hell. His entire world had crumbled. First the initial trickle of product returns followed by the flood of faulty merchandise coming back into his warehouse. Calls to the overseas manufacturer had proven futile, and to avoid destroying the name he'd worked so hard to build for himself he had to personally stand behind every last guarantee.

He'd stayed up late every night, going over flow-charts and budgets—seeing where he could cobble together the money needed to meet the demands of his unhappy customers. He hadn't wanted to worry Amira over it at the time, and he'd hoped he could cap the problem before it became overwhelming. Of course he hadn't counted on the newspaper spread announcing the recall of the product and his fall in fortune hitting the stands on the morning of the wedding. Nor had he counted on Amira reading the paper and deciding she didn't want to marry someone on the verge of bankruptcy after all.

Brent eased his foot off the accelerator and indicated to take a turn into a restricted parking area. She'd learn that you couldn't get away with treating other people like that. She wouldn't get to fool him again.

At the jewelers they were shown straight to a private room where the owner himself placed a series of small black velvet cases on the table between them. Brent watched Amira's face as one by one the owner opened each case and presented them to her for approval. He wasn't sure what he'd expected to see—some gleam of avarice, perhaps? But no, Amira remained as cool and composed as if she was presiding at a charity fund-raiser.

"What do you think, Brent? There are so many beautiful rings here. I'm finding it hard to choose."

She turned and gave him one of those serene smiles he recognized as the one she reserved for when she wasn't mentally engaged in what she was doing. The smile she'd perfected for the times when she was expected to front as her grandmother's puppet. And now she was his.

"What about this one?" he replied.

Brent deliberately reached over and picked the largest solitaire from its nest of velvet. Myriad sparks of color flew from it as the overhead lights refracted through the multiple facets. He took Amira's hand and slid the ring onto her finger. Her swiftly indrawn breath was the only indicator of her discomfort before she gracefully removed the ring and laid it back in its case.

"No, I don't think so."

"Perhaps something a little less overwhelming?" the jeweler suggested, sliding another case forward.

Inside was a princess cut diamond with tapered baguette diamonds set in the shoulders on each side. It was a beautiful piece.

Brent took the ring from the box and again put it on her finger. It was a perfect fit. The gold band hugged her finger, complementing the warm tone of her skin and the stones sparkled, showcased to their absolute brilliance in the setting.

"Yes, we'll take this one," he said without looking at Amira again. He couldn't when all he could remember right now was the night he'd given her first engagement ring to her. He'd planned every aspect of the evening in painstaking detail. He'd opted for simple and romantic over extravagance and had organized a picnic on a point of land overlooking Auckland City's inner harbor. As the sun had begun to set, he'd bent down on one knee and bared his heart and his love to her. He'd never believed he could be so happy when she said yes. Then again, he'd never believed she hadn't meant it.

"No!"

Her sharp denial dragged his attention back from the past.

"Why, what's wrong with it? It's a beautiful piece. Worth more than many people earn in a year."

"That's exactly what *is* wrong with it. You know the people I work with, the charities I serve. This...it's just too much. Too ostentatious. Do you have something simpler, with a colored stone perhaps?" She directed her question to the jeweler who, with a rueful look, unlocked a large wooden sliding drawer behind him and lifted a tray of rings from within.

"Perhaps one of these is more to your liking?" he inquired.

Brent sat back in his chair and watched Amira scan the assorted rings. Her eyes hovered over a section of aquamarines.

"Take those ones out," Brent instructed. "We'll look at them."

The jeweler lifted the section from the tray and returned the rest of the rings to the drawer, methodically locking it again.

"This one, I think," Amira said quietly as she picked up a smallish square-shaped aquamarine, with a sprinkling of tiny diamonds edging it.

"No," Brent interrupted her before she could try the ring on. "This one."

He reached across and lifted another ring, one with a much larger stone of the same cut and rimmed by white diamonds. He slid it on her finger and, holding her hand, turned it this way and that so the light caught on the stones.

"Sir, you've made a wonderful choice. It's a cushion

cut, just over five carats with excellent clarity, and the twenty-four surrounding stones—"

"It's too much," Amira protested.

"Look, you can tell your people it's fake for all I care," Brent said in a measured tone, totally ignoring the jeweler whose face had blanched at his words, "but you're my fiancée. You're wearing my ring. You think I want the world to see you wear something like this when you're going to be my wife?"

He gestured to the ring she'd selected, then picked up the obscenely large solitaire he'd chosen first and held it in front of Amira's face.

"This one?"

He lifted her hand to the same level.

"Or this. It's your choice."

Fake. The word rippled through her. Fake like their engagement. Fake like their marriage would be. Suddenly Amira felt as if she couldn't go through with this. It was all too much. It was one thing putting on a public face to the world but quite another when she'd have to maintain the same thing at home as well once they were married. There'd be no respite.

A stab of pain hit her square in the chest, and her fingers curled involuntarily around Brent's.

"Well? What's it going to be?" he demanded, not letting up an inch.

Amira wondered what the jeweler thought of their behavior. Hardly the usual thing one would expect from a newly engaged couple.

"This one. I'll take this one."

She pulled her hand from Brent's and stood, going to slide the ring from her finger.

"No, leave it. You may as well start wearing it straight away. We've got that charity ball to attend tonight, haven't we? Someone's bound to notice and set tongues wagging. Who knows, I might even manage to raise a couple more points on the exchange by morning."

There was an edge to his voice that sent a cold chill down Amira's spine. He flipped his platinum card from his wallet with a casualness that went a long way toward telling her how much he cared about what the ring had cost. His action would probably have been the same if she'd chosen the solitaire. Either way, price wasn't an issue for him.

She thought about how adamant he'd been that she select something showy and clearly expensive. Had he forgotten her so completely—forgotten that the trappings of wealth had never been what drove her?

After he'd completed the transaction, they walked out to their cars together.

"I'll see you tonight then," Amira said, depressing the electronic lock on her car key.

"Yes, I'll have my driver pick you up at eight."

"Your driver?"

Wasn't he coming to collect her himself? She had no wish to arrive at the hotel on her own. Certainly not with this pale-blue skating rink on her finger. It would be a struggle to maintain her poise when faced with the inevitable questions that would come her way.

"I'll meet you there. I have business in the city until about six so I've taken a room at the hotel to prepare."

"All right then. That will have to do."

As she drove away to her eleven o'clock appointment, she took a look in her rearview mirror. Brent stood there in the parking lot, dark sunglasses obscuring his eyes, which were undoubtedly still watching her.

A sensation of free-falling swept through her with stomach-lurching suddenness. This had all been her idea, but suddenly she didn't feel as though she was in control anymore. And control was vital to carry this through effectively. Otherwise, everything would have been in vain.

The black Mercedes-Benz E-Class V8 purred to a halt at the entrance to the hotel on Symonds Street, and Amira waited patiently for her door to be opened. As the door was held wide she swung her legs out and stood, allowing the sensuously soft fabric of her floor-length white silk gown to fall into its perfect lines. Elbow length white gloves had offered her the perfect foil for hiding her engagement ring, and she tugged them into place before adjusting the white faux fur stole she'd added to the ensemble at the last minute. She looked up as a large warm hand clasped hers.

"You're here," she remarked with a smile.

"I told you I'd be here," Brent said, drawing her closer. "Let's give them something to photograph, hmm?"

And just like that his lips were on hers. Amira's body surged to instant awareness as every nerve in her body jumped to attention. His lips were cool and soft as they pressed against hers. She leaned in toward him—drawn to his heat and strength like a bee to nectar—lost in the mastery of his lips.

It was over before it had begun, but it was no less devastating for all its brevity. Tiny tremors rocked her body as their vision was obscured by a mass of flashbulbs.

"Miss Forsythe, so it's true that your romance with Brent Colby has been rekindled?"

"How long have you been back together?"

"Amira! What would your grandmother think of your reunion?"

Questions flew from every direction—loud, confusing. Brent suavely directed Amira toward the front door and past the liveried doorman.

"Let's go inside. I think we've given them enough for one night, don't you?"

"Yes, definitely," Amira said, fighting to maintain her composure in the face of the barrage of questions.

With a smile painted firmly on her face she fought to keep her breathing even—a task harder than she anticipated as, with her hand firmly in the crook of Brent's arm, she and Brent entered the hotel lobby. She concentrated on the strength of the muscles in his forearm, on the fine cloth of his suit, on the enticing hint of his cologne that wafted by her as they stepped in unison toward the main ballroom.

"Pity we couldn't have timed the engagement announcement for tonight," Brent commented, bending his dark head to hers.

"No, we wouldn't have been able to sell the story if we made a public announcement at something like this. Not for as much anyway," Amira replied. "Marie said we should make the announcement next week, and I agreed."

Beneath her fingers she felt the muscles in his arm clench.

"I bow to your superior event management skills," he replied silkily, but Amira could tell her response had needled him.

So why not tell him the full story, she argued silently. What was stopping her from giving him the truth, lock, stock and two smoking barrels, about the foundation and what her grandmother had done to throw every obstacle in its way? About her promises to the children?

She swallowed against the lump in her throat. The lump that was pride and fear of failure blended with a burning desire to create a success in her life. Something that wasn't manufactured by her grandmother's influence. Something that was more than a tax break and could give hope to families from all over the country.

Something that, for the first time since she was ten years old, she could call her own.

Amira flicked a glance at his stern features. His dark brows were drawn in a straight line across his eyes— eyes that were more green than brown tonight as anger shone from them in unmistakable terms.

She quietly sighed. She'd made this rod for her back and she'd bear it. Brent was the only man she wanted at her side. Sure, she had considered other men for the role of her husband but she'd been telling Brent the truth when she'd said she didn't want any part of the accoutrements of marriage.

A coil of something undefined tightened deep inside her, giving the lie to her words. The truth was as startling to her as it was unexpected. The tension eased up a little, only to squeeze a tight band around her heart. Was it possible that she still hoped they could actually make a go of this fake marriage? That Brent could come to love her again? The thought rushed through her on a wave of exhilaration, only to be solidly dashed against the brick wall of the past. No, he'd never forgive her for what she did to him on their wedding day. Ever. He'd only entered into this sham relationship so he could further his already massive business enterprises. Expand his empire.

She'd entered this with her eyes and ears wide open. It would be tilting at windmills if she dared hope or dream for anything else. For once, Amira welcomed the pragmatism of her grandmother's influence and drew on every last ounce of it that she had in her personal armory.

If Brent caught so much as an inkling that she had entertained the thought of them creating a true marriage again she had no doubt he'd be laughing himself as far away from her as possible. Better that this should remain a charade, she consoled herself. That way no one would be hurt.

Six

As they drifted through the ballroom, Amira took the opportunity to introduce Brent to several members of the NZLB. As far as he was aware, his application to join was still under consideration, which basically meant he had to jump through these social hoops to move from consideration to the platinum level of membership she'd recommended. Would they make their decision tonight? He certainly hoped so.

Either way, it was worth the wait compared to how long he'd been stonewalled by all other aspects of his latest waterfront development. With the advent of the new performance arena, the scope for further business and parking in the surrounding area was huge. The sooner he could get his expansion project off the ground the better.

The band started to play, and several couples drifted onto the native timber parquet dance floor.

"Care to dance?" he murmured in Amira's ear.

She stiffened slightly, and for a moment he thought she'd refuse. But then with a regal incline of her head she accepted his request.

"Just give me a moment to put these down," she said, gesturing with her small silver clutch to her stole.

"Sure, would you like me to check them in or leave them at our table?"

"The table is fine. They're nothing of value."

Nothing of value? He'd lay odds each item had cost several hundred dollars. Her flippancy rankled. He pushed the irritation from his mind as he lifted the stole from her shoulders, inhaling a hint of her perfume as he did so. There it was again—that intriguing blend of spice and flowers. It hit him straight in the gut, sending all his instincts on full alert.

"I'll be just a minute," he said, taking her evening bag from her also.

The short respite of traveling the distance to their table and back to the edge of the dance floor allowed him to drag his wayward hormones under control. Business. He reminded himself. It was purely business. With a healthy dose of revenge, a little voice reminded him as he stepped up to Amira and took her hand, leading her to the dance floor.

She flowed into his arms as easily as if they did this sort of thing together every night. And in the old days they had, pretty much. When she'd come to visit him at his apartment he'd always had music playing in the background. Sometimes soft jazz, similar to what the band was playing tonight. Other times the gentle strains of a classical interlude. He loved music of any sort, but away from his office, or his social scene, he preferred to keep the sounds gentle and flowing. It helped to unwind at the end of a stressful day. All the easier when she'd been in his arms as well.

As far as female company was concerned, he'd been careful in the past years not to associate with any one woman more than twice in the public arena. He had no desire to be paired with someone in any shape or form for some time. Oh sure, one day he expected to marry and have a family. But he had a lot of work to do first.

And he had other matters to occupy his relaxation time these days, with the lap pool at his house he could enter into a punishing physical routine that scraped away every last vestige of a tough day at the office. Or he could get Draco or Adam for a vigorous game of tennis on his full-sized court.

He didn't need Amira and music in their subtle blend of seduction to calm him anymore. Although, as they swayed and moved to the music he felt his pulse kick up a beat, recognized the stirring in his loins that her proximity provoked.

She looked beautiful tonight. Every inch the consummate princess of style and charm. Her hair was twisted up tightly at the back of her head, exposing the graceful lines of her neck and the diamond drop earrings that fell from her earlobes. The tiny diamante straps that held her dress up appeared impossibly fragile, showcasing the curve of her shoulders with a feminine elegance that teased him to push them aside. To replace their caress with one of his own.

Brent reined in his thoughts, shifting his hips slightly away from Amira's. Before long he would lose control over his wayward flesh. Would show her exactly how much she attracted and tormented him still—and then who would have the edge?

Business. He reminded himself once more. Strictly business.

"Looks like the leaders of the NZLB are having a discussion together. Hopefully it's about your application," Amira said in a low voice, her breath a soft brush against his ear.

He turned his head slightly so he could see Auckland's most powerful collection of businessmen with their heads together over what looked like a bottle of fifty-year-old Chivas. One of the men laughingly gestured toward Amira and himself, and he carefully averted his gaze—but not before he'd seen the nods of approval from around the table.

"Looks promising, if they are indeed discussing my application," Brent replied.

"I think you have Uncle Don on your side. With his approval the others will soon follow suit."

"Uncle Don? I thought you didn't have any surviving family?"

He felt her stiffen in his arms and realised too late how painful his comment might have been.

"He's my godfather. His parents and my grandparents used to socialize together all the time, and he and my father were schoolmates. They lost touch when Mum and Dad married, and I haven't really seen him much over the years. But if he thinks that admitting you to the league will please me he'll lend his weight behind your application."

The music began to wind down and the emcee for the evening took the podium, inviting the guests to take their seats.

Brent fought the unexpected pang of physical loss as Amira peeled away from his side and led their return to their table. Their table partners were a mix of couples, one or two he'd met before, one he hadn't but was keen to foster a business relationship with.

As the evening drew on, Brent came to realize that Amira had probably planned it this way. She had, after all, been the one who directed the seating arrangements for the function and was due to assume the podium to make a short speech of thanks on behalf of the research charity the evening was a benefit for.

She managed everything with a finesse he reluctantly admired. No one would have realized how much work she'd put into the function from the way she laughed and conversed with their fellow guests—then maybe she hadn't done it all after all. Her type rarely did, he'd found over the years. With the backing of a strong support team they could still make their daily latte and air kiss sessions with their cronies at whichever Auckland café was the place of the week.

When it came time for Amira to make her speech, he watched as she rose and glided to the main stage. The deep low V of her gown showed a tantalizing glimpse of the soft curve of her lower back. She'd finally removed her gloves, and her long slender arms were bare. The overhead lighting on the stage caught the glint of her ring, and he smiled in satisfaction.

Brent flicked his gaze around the room. Yes, every man's eyes were on her. He tried to convince himself that he didn't feel the heated streak of possession that made him want to cover her body from their gaze, but he failed miserably.

It was ridiculous, he told himself. But then again, his reaction would certainly be expected if theirs was a real engagement, and to all intents and purposes it had to appear that way. To that end, he took delight when he caught the eye of one particularly lecherous watcher and gave him a narrow-eyed glare that clearly said "back off." He was deeply satisfied when the man gave him a nod of acknowledgment and then had the good grace to look away from Amira's tantalizing form.

This engagement might be business, Brent reminded himself, but there was a fair amount of game playing as well. And he was a consummate sportsman, no matter what the code. He sat back and listened as Amira thanked the sponsors for the evening and introduced the directors of the research charity, who she then called to the stage. Once everyone was lined up, she announced the total sum the evening had raised and presented a check to the directors.

As she came back and settled at the table, Brent leaned a little closer.

"You do that very well," he commented. "Even I was convinced you meant it."

"Of course I meant it. I'm not just a figurehead for these things you know. Whatever reasons Grandmother had for her involvement in her charities mine have never been in question."

"Helping those less fortunate than yourself?" Brent couldn't keep the edge of skepticism from his voice.

Amira's lips firmed in a straight line before she parted them to speak. "Yes, actually. Although that's no concern of yours."

He leaned closer. To anyone watching them it would look like a lover's private exchange.

"And all those millions you'll have at your disposal when you inherit? What do you plan to do with those? Come on, Amira. You don't expect me to believe this philanthropy is real—it's really just a game to you, isn't it? Something to fill your days. I bet you're looking forward to a *really* good time with all that money," he murmured.

Amira caught her breath at the veiled insult. She knew there were many people who only saw her for what she was—Isobel Forsythe's granddaughter—and not for who she was or how hard she worked behind the scenes. It had never really mattered to her before what others thought, so long as she did her job well.

Brent's comment, however, cut her deeply. His opinion of her must really be appallingly low. If that's how he felt, she was glad their marriage would be nothing but make-believe. It would be easier to hide her renascent feelings knowing he held her in such contempt.

"Well, you can never have enough, you know. Money, that is," she replied, even though the words felt like dry cereal in her mouth.

"Hear, hear." Brent lifted his champagne glass in a silent toast. "Thank you for being honest with me."

Honest? She'd always been honest with him. The only trouble was the one time she'd doubted her feelings for him, doubted her heart, it had turned out to be the biggest mistake of her life.

The rest of the evening passed successfully enough, rounding off with an invitation from the NZLB table inviting Brent and Amira to join them. With a raised brow, Brent accepted. Once Amira had introduced him to the men she made her apologies and withdrew. She'd done her part by sponsoring his application and by making the necessary introductions. Now it was up to him.

She checked with the hotel staff to make sure everything was progressing as it should for the evening and, with her back to the shadows, let her shoulders relax just a little. Only another hour and it would all be over tonight. Then she could put away her polished persona and relax in a warm bath before collapsing into bed.

She fingered the ring Brent had given her earlier today. How different it was from the simple diamond he'd given her the first time. How different their circumstances now. A pang of loss pulled at her heart. She'd been a fool to listen to Isobel that morning. A complete and utter fool. She should have known that Brent would

have had his reasons for not telling her of the collapse
of his business and finances. She should have trusted her
instincts that his attraction to her had never been about
her own perceived wealth.

If only he'd known, she thought bitterly. She was
entitled to nothing on her own apart from the payment
her parents' insurance policies had made available to her
on their deaths. A payment Isobel had topped up and set
instructions in place for it to end on Amira's thirtieth
birthday. Oh, sure, Isobel had imagined that Amira
would be well married by now, to some scion of New
Zealand business with a bank balance to match. But in
that, as in so many other things, Amira had failed her
grandmother again.

Sure she lived in the Forsythe Mansion and materi-
ally she wanted for nothing. However, nothing was
actually hers. The token stipends she was paid for her
work on the various charities Isobel had spearheaded
had been poured into the Fulfillment Foundation. If the
truth be known, she was probably in worse financial
position than Brent had been eight years ago.

Like him, she had her pride, if nothing else. She had
to succeed at this or acknowledge failure in every area
of her life. And, as far as she was concerned, that was
not an option.

The next morning the papers were live with speculation about the revival of Brent and Amira's romance.
As she sipped her morning cup of Earl Grey tea and
nibbled at her toast, Amira let a smile of satisfaction

spread across her face. In no time the calls would flood in from the women's magazines—each one wanting an exclusive. Maybe she'd even be able to forestall Caroline's departure if she could cover back pay and at least the next couple of months' wages.

For a moment she wished they'd brought the wedding closer but then quickly discarded the idea out of hand. They couldn't be seen rushing things or it would arouse suspicion. Certainly the few short months they'd agreed upon could be seen to be acceptable. And then there'd be the wedding pictures to sell as well.

A warm glow started deep inside at the thought of being able to tell Casey and her new family when they'd be going to Disneyland. It would make everything worthwhile. Even the pain of being in a loveless marriage to a man who despised her.

With the anticipated calls of the magazines in mind, Amira changed her voice mail message on her machine, directing all inquiries to her publicist. That itself would confirm the rumors of an engagement she'd seen in one of the papers.

She wondered how Brent was faring this morning. It would probably pay to have him put the same message on his voice mail as well. She picked up the phone and dialed his number.

"Colby," he answered, his tone clipped.

"Brent, good morning. I trust you slept well now that your development will be going ahead sooner than you anticipated?"

Before they'd left last night he'd told her that the league had accepted him into their exalted establishment and had assured him of their support with his current venture.

"Yes, thank you. I did sleep well, although I could have done without the string of photographers along the estuary walkway when I went for my morning run." He sounded rueful. "I think until things die down a bit I'll stick to my home gym. It was time I updated the treadmill anyway. How about you? Pleased with how last night went?"

As she replied in the affirmative, it struck her how empty their conversation was. As if between colleagues, not people who the world would soon believe were lovers. Their engagement was a hollow victory but a victory nonetheless she reminded herself.

"You might want to put a message on your voice mail directing everyone to Marie. As our publicist she'll relish handling all that side of things."

"Good idea."

"By the way, I don't have any official functions on my calendar for this week. I was thinking it might whet people's appetites for news if we're not seen together quite as much. What do you think?"

He hesitated a while before answering. Amira had no trouble imagining the expression on his face as he pondered her suggestion. No doubt he'd be thinking she had a hidden agenda. And maybe she did. A part of her wondered if it would simply be easier not to be reminded daily of what she'd thrown away when she stood him up—be easier not to be reminded of how artificial her life had become.

"Sure, that works for me. With the waterfront job coming together I'll be pretty full on this week anyway."

Amira regretted her suggestion the moment they said goodbye and she hung up her phone. She'd thought it would be easier. In reality she welcomed any excuse to see him, to touch him—even if it was only for show. Now she had no excuse to see him during the week, and by his own admission he was busy.

She'd just have to fill her time with other matters, she decided. By the end of the week, Marie had been approached by the major weekly glossy magazines for the rights to an exclusive interview with Brent and Amira. The staggering sums they offered were all much the same with various additional incentives thrown in to sweeten the individual pots.

"So what do you two think? Which magazine do you want to go with?" Marie asked as she stepped back from Brent's desk where she'd laid out the different offers they'd received.

"Who has the highest circulation?" Brent asked, his face a noncommittal mask.

"This one," Marie pointed to one of the offers.

"Then we should go with them," he replied.

"No," Amira interjected as Marie started to gather up the papers.

"You'd rather go with someone else?" Marie asked.

Amira straightened in her seat, avoiding Brent's gaze as she chose her words carefully. No matter what she said, no matter how this came out, he'd still think badly of her. She thought about those wages, about the strain her staff was under.

"I'm not satisfied they're offering enough. Why don't we play them off one another, like an auction?" she asked.

"An auction—I haven't coordinated one of those before." Marie paced back and forth a few times, her brow furrowed in concentration. "I think you're right, Miss Forsythe. We could definitely lever this higher. I know you vetoed mentioning your past engagement, but I'm thinking we might need to offer them more, perhaps something about why you two split in the first place…?"

Brent rose from his chair in a flood of movement. He gave Amira a cold, hard look.

"Is that what you want? To rake over old coals to get more money?"

His voice could freeze Lake Taupo solid, Amira thought as she gathered her strength to her.

"If that's what it takes to drive up the price, yes."

A light seemed to die in Brent's eyes.

"Then do what you must."

Marie looked from one to the other. "Oh-kay, I'll get onto this right away then and get back to you as soon as I have a plan together."

"Thank you, Marie," Amira said, her gaze not moving from Brent's set features.

"I'll let myself out."

When Marie had gone Amira spoke.

"I hope this change in plans doesn't make you want to pull out of the interview."

"I'll show up for the interview no matter what you've arranged. Just know that I don't believe you need to do this, Amira."

"Believe me, I do."

His expression said it all. He thought she was nothing more than a money-hungry greed machine. He sighed and wiped his hand across his eyes.

"When will it be enough?"

"Don't you know? It's never enough. Not for people like me." She managed a brittle laugh to cover the hurt she felt inside at the disgust on his face. She could never tell him the truth of her grandmother's hold over her. That even as Isobel's closest blood relative she'd never been good enough to win the old lady's heart, nor the unstinting support that should have been hers by right. That she'd always been held up as an example of her parents' failures to provide for her properly.

"You know, I'd actually feel sorry for you if I didn't think it was a total waste of time."

"I've never asked anyone to feel sorry for me," Amira replied, injecting steel into her tone. "I do what I have to do, when I have to do it."

"That you do." Brent turned away from her, his hands clasped at his back as he faced out the window to the estuary beyond. "Is that all for today? I think you should go."

"Fine, I'll be in touch after I've heard from Marie."

He didn't so much as nod in acknowledgment as she left the room, and inside she felt as if another piece of her soul had been shaved away.

Seven

The interview with the women's magazine went extremely well, and the photo spread showed exactly what it should—a couple in love, with a second chance at happiness.

Amira dropped her copy of the magazine on her coffee table. So why didn't she feel happy? The publication had sold out within hours of reaching the newsstands and supermarket stands, and Marie had fielded offers from Australia to feature their article there also.

She should be dancing for joy. The money from the interview had already been deposited in the foundation's account, and the staff's wages had been paid, together with a generous bonus for their loyalty. Amira pressed a knotted fist against her chest. The hollow ache inside never went away; instead it grew ever more painful.

The smiling couple on the front cover of the glossy magazine didn't seem real. Maybe that's because they weren't real, she reminded herself.

And maybe how she was feeling was due in part to the legal envelope that had been delivered by courier to her here at home the other day. The prenuptial agreement she'd suggested Brent have his lawyer draw up. She'd skimmed through it, then signed and returned it. Oh sure, she knew she should have had her own lawyers give independent legal advice on the document before signing, but it was pretty basic really.

The terms had been set out in black and white. In return for agreeing to marry her, Amira would see to it that Brent received the platinum level entry into the NZLB as she'd promised, together with a sum of money being not less than ten percent of the amount she would inherit under her grandmother's estate upon marriage. She didn't see how it could be any simpler. Gerald Stein, the family lawyer, would probably have a heart attack if he knew what she'd just done, but he'd still been away on a much-needed extended vacation, touring the cathedrals of Europe. Besides, she had taken control of her life.

She had offered those very things, Brent had agreed, and now their engagement was out there for all the world to see. Of course all the world also meant that no doubt Roland would soon know that his plans to move into the Forsythe mansion were in imminent danger of being thwarted. She wondered what type of message he'd take to leaving on her machine then. Thank heavens for caller ID.

As if the mere thought of the phone triggered it to ring, it suddenly shrilled in the quiet of her apartment. Despite herself, Amira jumped, her heart racing in her chest. A quick check of the screen confirmed it wasn't Roland, and with a brief sigh of relief she recognized Gerald Stein's private number.

"Gerald, how are you? How was your holiday?"

"Wonderful, thank you. But tell me, child, what on earth have you been up to? We must talk—urgently."

There was a note to Gerald's voice that instantly set Amira's nerves on edge. She drew a deep breath before answering.

"Up to, Gerald? Why, fulfilling the terms of grandmother's will. I suppose you've seen the news."

"Exactly. Look, it's vital I talk to you before you do anything else, and please, give no more interviews or statements to the press until we've spoken. I'll have Cynthia clear a spot for you at three thirty. See you then."

Without even waiting for her affirmative he hung up, leaving Amira with a disconnected beep in her ear and a puzzled frown on her face. She'd never known Gerald to be so abrupt, nor to sound quite so harried. Not even when Isobel had passed away, and the two of them had gone way back. In fact, Amira had often wondered if their relationship had ever proceeded beyond the professional boundaries of lawyer and client.

Whatever had happened in the past, it was her future that needed her full attention right now. Amira checked her PDA and made a few quick phone calls to rearrange things so she could make her meeting with Gerald.

She dressed conservatively for the meeting, wearing a pale pink silk blouse under a black suit with a knee-length pencil skirt. Patent black leather high-heeled pumps matched her slim bag to complete the ensemble. She tied her hair back in a long braid that fell down her back in a straight line, bumping against her spine as she walked.

The offices of Stein, Stein & Stein were located in the heart of Auckland City, in one of the few remaining heritage buildings on Queen Street, which resisted full modernization and clung tenaciously to its splendor of yesteryear. As a child she'd always been fascinated by the old wooden paneling that lined the corridors leading to the partners' offices. On those rare occasions that Isobel had brought her into town, it had always been a treat of magnificent dimensions to take tea with Gerald in his office. Now, of course, Amira realized how narrow her world had been. Her every step guided by her grandmother, her every behavior constantly monitored. Still, as structured as her life had been, it had stood her in good stead. Now she could face down a battalion of New Zealand's elite and coax sponsorship from them. For all but the Fulfillment Foundation, anyway.

She wondered whether Gerald's call was related to the problems she'd had with paying the staff. His firm handled the legal issues on behalf of the foundation and had seen to its registration as a charitable trust. But what if someone had brought a grievance against her or the foundation? A deep sense of misgiving plucked at the back of Amira's mind.

Gerald didn't waste time getting to the point of their meeting. He was blunt and to the point.

"You have to call off your engagement."

"Call off my engagement? But why? Gerald, you know I have to marry to inherit. Brent and I have come to an arrangement with which we're both extremely comfortable."

Okay, so maybe that was a slight exaggeration, she admitted silently. But they had made an arrangement. An arrangement she would abide by no matter how much it played on her mind, and no matter how much she now wished it could have been based on mutual respect and even love.

"It's impossible. I'm sorry, my dear, but you have no choice." A worried frown settled over his watery blue eyes, and he adjusted his glasses on his nose as he reached for the papers lying in front of him on the desk.

"But I don't understand. You told me that I had to marry to inherit under grandmother's will. That's exactly what I'm doing, in," she said while mentally counting off the calendar, "eight weeks' time."

"I can assure you, if you're going to inherit you will not be marrying Brent Colby in eight weeks' time." He swiped his glasses off his nose and cleaned them with a tissue before settling them back on. "Your grandmother was quite explicit. I never saw the need to tell you about her proviso because I never dreamed you and Colby would get back together. You know how Isobel felt about him. And, of course, after your failed wedding…well, enough said about that. Suffice to say I chose not to inform you of these terms because I didn't believe in waking sleeping dogs. Especially not hard on the heels of your bereavement. That said, I've done you a great disservice. I'm terribly sorry, my dear."

A disservice? He'd withheld a vital piece of her grandmother's will from her. And all because he hadn't wanted to upset her? An icy trickle of dread ran down Amira's spine. What had Isobel put in place that meant she had to break off her engagement with Brent?

"What proviso?" she said quietly.

"Now, you know your grandmother only had your best interests at heart."

"Tell me about the proviso," she insisted in a voice that brooked no further argument.

"Right. Yes. Of course." The elderly solicitor shuffled the papers before him and lifted one page. He cleared his throat then began to read. "And I furthermore direct that under no circumstances will my granddaughter, Amira Camille Forsythe, inherit if she should resume her previous relationship with the said Brent Colby, or if she should marry him."

Amira's heart twisted painfully. This was unbelievable. Her mind struggled to comprehend the ramifications of Gerald's words even as the sound of his voice died on the air. How could Isobel have made such an outrageous demand? Wasn't it bad enough that she'd used emotional blackmail to force Amira to withdraw from marrying him eight years ago? And that now, from her grave, she was forcing Amira to marry *anyone* else?

"Surely that won't withstand a challenge." Amira finally managed through lips that felt stiff and frozen.

"It may, and it may not. Either way, do you really have the time to devote to a challenge through the court? And, my dear, while I hate to remind you of this, do you really have the funds at your disposal to mount such a challenge?"

She hadn't believed it could get much worse, but Gerald's words were the death knell to her plans. There was no way she'd be able to fund such a legal challenge even if it could be pushed through the court system with any haste. Her body slumped in the deep leather wing chair where she'd perched so many times, legs swinging happily, as a child. The contrast between then and now had never been so evident.

Who would have thought her life would come to this? A marionette still being manipulated by a domineering old woman. Her breath shuddered in her lungs as the enormity of her grandmother's reach clutched deathly fingers around her dream and wrenched it from the realms of possibility.

"Amira?" Gerald interrupted her thoughts. "I know this has come as a shock to you, but may I remind you of the alternative?"

A cynical laugh fought its way past the lump in her throat.

"What? Bankruptcy? Living on the streets?"

She couldn't help it, but right now no other solution

presented itself. It wasn't just about the money, no matter what Brent thought of her in that regard, although without the money from her inheritance the foundation would be lost forever—closed due to mismanagement and insufficient funds. And it would be all her fault. All those lost dreams, not to mention the loss of employment for her staff.

How would she explain it to the children and their parents? How would she break the news to Casey? A sob rose in her throat, but she swallowed against it, instead closing her eyes for a moment and pushing down the urge to cry out in desperation. Why was it that as soon as one door opened in her life another slammed viciously shut just as quickly?

And how was she to break the news to Brent? Would he ever understand or forgive her now that she was forced to jilt him again? Tears burned harshly at the back of her eyes, and she closed them again, determined not to let go.

Gerald cleared his throat uncomfortably. For a man who'd just come back from a lengthy holiday, he already looked strained and gray with stress.

"I don't wish to be indelicate, but do you recall the other part to this inheritance clause in Isobel's will?"

"Other part?" Amira's mind refused to budge from the death of her hopes for the future.

Gerald shuffled through the copy of the will on his desk and stabbed a stubby finger at the paper. "Yes, this one. This subclause relating to having borne live issue before your thirtieth birthday." Gerald sounded as uncomfortable suggesting it as he obviously felt if the way he ducked his head and fidgeted with his papers was anything to go by.

A child? How on earth would she find someone to father a child when all she wanted was what was rightfully hers? And how did one go about that sort of thing anyway? Brent was out of the question. Once he knew she had to break off their engagement again there was no way on this earth he'd touch her, let alone give her a child, even if they hadn't agreed to keep their relationship purely on a business footing.

Which left what? A sperm donor? A one-night stand and hope for a hit? Her mind instantly rejected both options as impossible. She could no more submit to a coldly clinical procedure using donor sperm to bring a baby into the world, for the sheer purpose of inheriting, than she could fly off the Auckland Sky Tower. Nor could she subject herself, or her theoretical child, to the dangers of a one-night stand.

No. If she was to have any man's child, by choice, it would be Brent's. Which left only one option.

One man.

Could she carry it off? Could she withhold the truth from him that she was going to jilt him again for long enough to get him to father a child with her?

Amira's stomach churned at the thought of using him so cold-bloodedly. But would it be cold-blooded? They'd had a passionate relationship before. Could she hope to stoke that fire of attraction between them again to trick him into impregnating her?

She thought of little Casey—a child to whom life had already dealt too many blows with the loss of her family and her leukemia. She thought of the many other children being added to the register of the Fulfillment Foundation. Of the families desperate for some respite or hope—families who deserved so much more than the months and years of unhappiness they'd been dealt through circumstance.

A picture of Roland's dissolute features swam into her mind, together with the latest gossip headlines from Australia, which speculated over the size of his gambling debt, his hard drinking and loose women. And she knew she had to do it. She had to seduce Brent to have his baby.

Eight

"Two to one odds. Not bad," Adam commented over the rim of his brandy balloon as he watched Brent line up a shot on the billiard table. "But I like your odds better. I'm thinking I might place a bet. What do you reckon?"

Despite Adam's attempt to distract him, Brent pocketed the brown and set up his next shot. The wide-screen LCD TV mounted on the wall opposite them droned on. Not satisfied with touting two to one odds that Amira wouldn't show up on the day, the cohost on the late night show that was screening had offered ten to one odds that it would be Brent who'd fail to show.

"I reckon you should keep your money in your pocket," Brent answered, hoping his cousin would drop the subject. He should be so lucky. "Or at least place a decent bet on this game."

Adam just laughed. "C'mon, Brent. You know you have no intention of going through with this. Can't a man have a little fun along the way? It's not as if I'm likely to make any money off you tonight any other way, what with Draco AWOL and—"

"It's not a joke, Adam," Brent said quietly.

"Yeah, I know. She cut you up pretty bad last time. So, how's it going anyway? You guys are spending a lot of time together. Mending any bridges?"

Brent chalked the tip of his cue. Mending bridges? No. Not a chance. But he was making some inroads at getting under her skin. He thought back to the brief montage of clips they'd shown on the late night talk show. One in particular had shown Amira in an unguarded moment, and the hunger on her face as she'd looked at him had been unmistakable.

"I don't know about bridges, but she's asked me to Windsong this weekend."

Adam sat up in his chair. "*The* Windsong? The Forsythe private hideaway? My, my, things are looking up."

Brent laughed. Looking up or not, he planned to have Amira in his bed by the end of the weekend. He wanted her bound to him in every way possible. That way, when he cut her loose, she'd get a taste of what he'd gone through eight years ago.

"Well," Adam said as Brent finished off the table, "as scintillating as your company is, I'd better be on my way. Have a few problems of my own to sort out."

"Anything I can help you with?"

"No, I can handle it. This one's right up my alley. Or at least she will be, eventually." He gave Brent a wink and grabbed his car keys from the coffee table. "Thanks for dinner. We'll have to try and track down Draco and pin the next meal on him. It's not like him to miss these nights when he's back in New Zealand. Do you think it has anything to do with that woman at the memorial service?"

"Who knows, but if it is, I can't wait to hear why. If he calls, I'll let you know."

"Same," Adam agreed.

After he'd seen Adam off, Brent wandered back in to the game room. The late show was still going on about him and Amira. He flicked a finger on the remote to turn off the TV. Couldn't anyone talk about anything these days but the upcoming nuptials of the Forsythe Princess and the Midas Man, as they'd dubbed him in the national papers during recent years?

He took a sip of his brandy, but the entertainment slot had soured his taste buds. The Midas Man. They trotted out nicknames with unerring frequency and with no small amount of irritation to the recipient. There was nothing golden in his touch. Everything he'd gained he'd achieved through sheer bullheadedness and damn hard work. And he'd done it alone.

Alone. The word echoed through his mind. How different would their life have been had she gone through with their first planned wedding? Would she still be at his side? Would they have started a family by now, the halls of the house echoing with the sounds of children at play?

He pushed the thoughts from his mind. It was time wasted dwelling on an impossible past. He hadn't made his fortune by looking back.

He thought ahead to tomorrow's meeting with Amira and Marie and of the matters they needed to discuss. Topping the list was some way of getting Marie to generate counterpublicity to the current reign of conjecture as to whether or not Amira would actually make it to the altar this time. For his own satisfaction he wanted to put a lid on any comment that she might not make it.

Above all, the last thing he needed was some magazine to run a story expounding on the theory he might be the one to pull out this time. He didn't need her to be spooked at this stage of things. Mind you, with the carrot of her inheritance dangling juicily in front of her he'd wager the better part of his fortune that there was no way she'd be standing him up this time.

It niggled at him constantly, this avaricious need of hers to gather more and more funds. The subsidiary rights to their engagement and reunion story had sold for an exorbitant sum, a sum he had no doubt that she'd drummed up as high as she could get it.

She'd never been this focused on money before, never been this…greedy. The word had a nasty sound to it, one totally at odds with the Amira he'd fallen in love with the first time around. But that woman had been phony, he reminded himself—as phony as his intention to follow through with their wedding now. It occurred to him that when he didn't turn up at the wedding she'd no doubt sell that story to the highest bidder too.

It was an irony that wasn't entirely wasted on him, and a smile curled his lips as he switched off the downstairs lights and made his way upstairs to the master suite.

Her uncharacteristic grasping need for disposable income had sent up a few flags in his mind, and he had called in one of his handpicked private investigators to do some digging to find out what lay behind the apparent change in Amira's fortune. With her father having been the only, and much beloved, child of the old dragon and her husband, Amira stood to gain a lot from Isobel's passing. Unless there was more to it than Amira had said. If that was the case, he'd soon know all there was to know.

He thought about her elegant beauty at the charity function the other week—the night he'd received his formal invitation to the league. She'd carried the whole evening off with a sophistication totally at odds with her current financial obsession.

When the car had pulled up in the forecourt of the hotel and he'd stepped forward to assist her from her seat, his heart had slammed against his chest at the sight of her. Every instinct in him had fought, with untamed need, to sweep her past the ballroom entrance and instead to the suite he'd used to prepare for the evening. And there he wanted to slake the simmering lust for her that glowed, silent and hungry, beneath the surface of his composure.

Damned if she didn't still push all his buttons to high alert every time he saw her. It was a situation he'd expected to have mastered by now, to have wrestled under control. But instead it only seemed to gather strength. To burn hotter, harder.

He should never have agreed to her terms of a strict business arrangement. He'd entered into this too lightly—too intent on extracting his own revenge against the only woman he had ever loved. He hadn't stopped to weigh the cost, physical or mental. And right now that physical cost was tying him in knots. There hadn't been a single night in this past week where he hadn't woken, sheets tangled about him, his body raging with a fever only Amira could assuage. Tonight would be no different. It augured badly for the next couple of months, but he could and would tolerate it if it meant he'd get to teach her that overdue lesson. To show her you couldn't walk all over people the way she'd walked all over him.

The next morning an e-mail from his private investigator awaited him. He was surprised to get a response so swiftly, but the content of the e-mail surprised him more. Surprised and concerned him.

Amira Forsythe was, to date, the sole donor to and benefactor of the Fulfilment Foundation. He'd heard of the foundation and of Amira's work with it. He'd assumed that, as usual, she was a figurehead—no more than an attractive spokesperson whose primary function was to attract sponsorship and public interest with her already high profile. Further details followed on the mission statement of the foundation and its charter. Brent found himself agreeing to its core structure and overall purpose, but he was horrified when he saw the projected costs to run the foundation and its current financial position.

Where was the money Amira's family were famous for bestowing on the charities of their choice? He could name at least ten charities, without even straining his memory, the Forsythes publicly supported in varying degrees. So why not this one?

By the looks of things, it was Amira's baby.

He poured himself a fresh cup of coffee and continued reading the report. Further digging had shown that Isobel had been outspoken amongst her peers about the infeasibility of the foundation—a fact that puzzled Brent. Why this one? Was the old lady so determined to control everything Amira did that she'd quashed her granddaughter's ideas? The fact Amira had gone ahead and set up the foundation and put things in motion to implement its plans showed backbone he'd never witnessed in her before.

The next paragraph had him replace his mug carefully on his desk and whistle long and low. How his PI had garnered this particular snippet of information he really didn't want to know. It went deeper into the Forsythe financial structure than Brent would have imagined possible, even with the exorbitant sum he paid the PI. The guy had definitely earned himself a generous bonus.

Apparently Amira had no personal income—only a small annuity from her parents' life insurance. An annuity that her grandmother had topped up in keeping with inflation—a fact her parents had sadly neglected to consider, obviously, when they'd taken out their policies. Worse, the annuity, which appeared to be channeled directly into the foundation, was due to cease on Amira's thirtieth birthday.

How on earth did the foundation function? The donations from the general public were abysmally low. Without major sponsorship or generosity from a clutch of private donors, the entire thing would collapse around her ears. How could she play with people's lives like that? To all accounts and purposes she was virtually promising these children and their families the moon; yet all she could deliver was a handful of space dust.

A slow burning anger rose from Brent's gut, making his vision blur and his hands clench into fists on the desktop. Just how irresponsible could Amira be? He knew what it was like to do without and what it was like to have to accept financial aid to achieve his potential.

Sure, he'd paid back every penny his uncle had put forward, but without that money in the first place, he'd never have had the opportunity to attend Ashurst and even earn the scholarship that had made repayment possible. Whatever people said, money moved mountains. Not having it made people vulnerable and the Fulfillment Foundation was there for the most vulnerable of all.

The foundation promised scholarships, family holidays—all manner of things that any child or family could wish for. Hadn't these people suffered enough without added disappointment? Did Amira have no idea of the amount of pride it took to accept a handout, or any inkling as to what it would feel like to see that pride trodden upon when the promise was broken?

Amira had been given opportunities galore in her life and yet she was still as flippant with others as she'd been with her promise to marry him—to love him. Obviously the foundation was nothing more than a passing interest to her. A game. It made him feel ill to see how she had trivialized something so important.

He could make a difference to this charity. He could help these people reach for their dreams, see the children involved know happiness where before they'd only known illness and hardship. His mind began ticking off the possibilities and he opened a new e-mail, to both his accountant and his lawyer, listing a series of instructions.

The Fulfillment Foundation would reach its potential, eventually. But one thing was certain. Amira Forsythe would not be at its helm when it did so.

Amira paced the confines of her sitting room. A baby. She had to have a baby with Brent. She laid her hand on her stomach. What would it be like to bring his child into the world? A flush of heat spread through her body. What would it be like to be back in his arms—in his bed? Her womb tightened, sending a spiral of longing through her body. Her breasts suddenly heavy, sensitive to the softness of her silk bra, the tease of lace across the demi cup.

She remembered the touch of his hands, the taste of his skin, the heat of his possession with a primitive longing that made her groan out loud in the pristine silence of the room. She fisted her hand to her mouth. God, how on earth would she get through this?

She had eight weeks—only eight weeks—to pull it off. A quick check last night of her last menstrual cycle, thankfully always as regular as clockwork, showed her prime time to conceive would probably fall over the coming weekend. If that didn't work out she had one more chance and then, if that failed also, nothing.

Would she be lucky enough to get pregnant right away? She'd heard so many stories of women who'd struggled for years to become pregnant.

This was monumental. The decision to make a child, to bring a helpless baby into the world for any reason other than out of love went against everything she'd ever believed in. Everything she'd ever hoped for. But the thought of holding her child in her arms. Someone who was hers. Someone who didn't judge, didn't find fault, didn't find her wanting. The concept was almost overwhelming.

She was getting ahead of herself. First she had to swing it. She had to coerce Brent into her bed and convince him to have unprotected sex with her. She had to ruthlessly lie and use him—seduce him into making love with her, sharing breath, sharing each other's bodies.

Again her body tightened, thrummed in anticipation. It would take some planning, but planning was what she was good at. And she had the means and the motivation to get him there; all it would take was a little subtlety, some nuance. She could do this. She had to.

He'd never forgive her when he found out. A fine tremor ran through her body. He'd be angry. Far more angry than when she'd left him standing at the altar. But she'd gladly bear his anger to honor her promise to the children. Gladly bear his child.

It all seemed so clinical. So unfair. What had her grandmother been thinking when she'd inserted that wretched clause in her will? Not of Amira's happiness, certainly. But then had her happiness ever been Isobel's primary focus? Amira scoured her memories.

She had grown up desperate for some measure of affection from Isobel, always striving for her approval—almost trying to make up to her grandmother for her parent's failings. With the charity work she'd begun to believe she'd finally achieved that goal, until Isobel had dismissed her plans with the Fulfillment Foundation.

What made a woman so bitter that she didn't want to invoke hope in others? Was duty everything?

Right now it was. It was Amira's duty to the beneficiaries of the foundation to have that baby, no matter how cold-blooded its need for conception.

Her heart turned over in her chest. How could she do this? After her own upbringing she'd made a fervent promise to any future child of hers that they would know the joy of being loved by two parents, as she had even if it was short-lived.

But then the question raised itself in her mind. How could she not? Once she inherited and the foundation was set up in perpetuity she could manage quite nicely on a small but solid base of investment income. Even after she paid Brent what she'd promised, her baby would want for nothing.

Nothing but parents who loved each other.

Children all over the world were brought up in single parent families, she argued with herself. And it wasn't as if she knew for certain that Brent would reject their baby, in fact she very much doubted he would. She could even end up with a major battle on her hands for custody if truth be told.

Well, she'd cross that bridge if and when she came to it, she decided. Right now, the most important thing was getting pregnant.

Nine

On Saturday morning Amira stood at the end of the jetty and tried to breathe evenly. Anything to settle the butterflies that lurched about like crazed winged beasts in her stomach. She still couldn't believe he'd agreed to this respite weekend at Windsong.

The private cove and beach had been in the family for generations. One rustic dwelling replaced by another until the current two-storied plantation-style home was constructed during Isobel's reign. With access only by air or by sea, the property was intensely private, and the small staff employed to keep the house and grounds in pristine condition lived on the outskirts of its expansive boundaries.

The wind rustled through the phoenix palms that

lined the front of the house where it faced the sea, the sound reaching out to where Amira waited. Warm air circulated around her, caressing her bare midriff beneath the knotted white muslin blouse she wore above an ankle length cotton skirt. The well-worn fabrics pressed against the outline of her body in the breeze, and she was forced to hold on to the cowboy-style sun hat she'd perched on her head when she'd received the radio call from the launch's skipper to say they were ten minutes away from docking.

Clouds gathered in the sky, beginning to chase away the glorious sunshine that had bathed the island since sunrise this morning. The rain, when it came, would force them indoors.

A shiver of anticipation rolled through Amira's body, echoed by a thrill of excitement as the launch cleared the point and swooped in a semicircle toward the jetty. This was it. He was here. Everything now hinged on the success of today, and tonight. Just one night, but oh, the possibilities were endless.

She'd panicked a little when he'd called off from coming over to the island yesterday, being Friday, saying a problem at work would keep him late. But she consoled herself that she still had tonight and even all day tomorrow if everything went to plan. It had to be enough.

She could see him now, on the flying bridge next to the skipper, his short dark hair ruffling in the breeze. Dark sunglasses shaded his eyes, and his face was an unreadable mask from this distance.

Suddenly she couldn't wait for him to disembark. To be able to reach out, to touch him.

But she couldn't rush things. With the way they'd structured their arrangement, physical contact had been limited. The kiss he'd given her at the hotel a couple of weeks ago had been the only public display of affection to date, although he'd made a habit of using a proprietary touch when they were out. As if he was staking a silent claim. That said, to rush things now might throw her plans into total disarray.

She swept her hat off her head and her fingers clenched into the straw brim. It was too important that everything go off perfectly. She had to stick to her plans. To tantalize. To tease. Until falling into one another's arms was the most natural thing in the world, and the chasm of the past that lay between them could cease to exist for awhile.

Brent felt an all too familiar clutch in his gut when he saw Amira standing on the jetty waiting for the launch to dock. There was a casual relaxed air about her, as if here she was a different person to the one he'd squired around to Auckland's major functions in the past few weeks. Even what she was wearing was more like the old Amira. Just how many faces did she have? Once, a long time ago, he'd thought he knew her. The only thing he was certain of now was that he most certainly didn't.

Nor did he trust her. Not after discovering the financial mess that was the background of the foundation.

Her invitation to come out to Windsong for the weekend had intrigued him, even though she'd made the suggestion on the pretext of finalizing their wedding plans and guest list without interruption or distraction from their work. There were no paparazzi here, no gossip columnists. Altogether no financial advantage to them being together, aside from the fact that it was the kind of thing a normal engaged couple might do.

Except they weren't that kind of normal.

His mouth twisted in a wry smile. She was up to something again. Maybe it was the late night talk show earlier this week that had headlined the odds of their wedding going ahead that had spooked her. Perhaps it had been enough to make her want to assure Brent of her intention to follow through on the day, or even assure herself of his.

His gaze swept up past the palm trees and the immaculately manicured lawns preceding the pillared front of the house. He'd never been invited here before but he'd heard a great deal about the place. Why anyone needed a weekend retreat with nine bedrooms and six bathrooms, not to mention two offices, was beyond him. But then old Isobel had always known how to make an impression.

The launch bumped gently against the rubber bumpers on the jetty and, with a quiet word of thanks to the skipper, Brent skimmed down the stairs from the flying bridge. He collected his overnight bag from in the main cabin then stepped off the transom at the rear and onto the jetty where Amira waited.

Instantly every cell in his body went on full alert. Her skin still carried the golden blush of summer, and he couldn't help but let his eyes skim over her—from the deep exposed V of her blouse to where it knotted beneath her full breasts and then below to her bare midriff. Instinctively, he reached out, traced a finger across the soft curve of her belly.

He pulled his hand away, but not before he felt the answering quiver across her skin.

"Shall we go to the house? I've prepared some breakfast. You haven't eaten already, have you?"

"No. Sure, lead the way."

Amira prepared breakfast? Didn't she have staff here, he wondered. He stayed slightly behind her as she walked along the narrow jetty, her bare feet making next to no sound on the smooth weathered boards. Her hips swayed slightly as she took each step, and he felt heat rise under the collar of his shirt. Damn, if he didn't know better he would think she was deliberately enticing him. He drew level to her as they crossed the lawn to the house.

"Would you like to put your things away first?" Amira asked as they entered the spacious front foyer.

"Yeah, that'd be great."

Her warm friendliness had him on the back foot. He'd grown used to her being the cool ice princess she was renowned for. Cool, icy and avaricious.

Upstairs, the room she showed him was huge. A super-king-sized bed, clad in coffee-colored linens that matched the walls and contrasted perfectly with the creamy colored carpet, took pride of place against one wall in the room. Opposite, French doors opened out onto a wide balcony with a view of the bay.

"Nice room," he commented.

"It's the master. I thought you'd be comfortable here."

"You don't use this room yourself?"

"I have my own room just down the hall," Amira answered, bending forward to smooth an imaginary ripple out of the bed covering.

He hadn't been certain she wasn't wearing a bra beneath her blouse before, but now he was. Painfully certain. She bent forward a little farther, unwittingly exposing another inch of sun-gilded skin and just a hint of a dusky pink nipple. His body went rock hard. He dropped his weekend bag on a large chest at the foot of the bed and grabbed his toilet bag from inside. Determined to put some space between them, he strode through to the ensuite bathroom she'd shown him and put his things on the cream-colored marble vanity.

Coming over for this weekend worked in well with his plans. When he dashed her hopes of marriage he wanted her in his thrall. Physically and emotionally. While she'd strived to maintain an emotional distance since they'd been back together, he'd sensed that under the surface she wasn't quite as cool as she portrayed. No matter how he'd orchestrated her comeuppance, she was still a mightily attractive woman. A fact his libido had taken note of more than once. This craving for her had become a constant. Taking it to the next level would be no hardship.

A small sound from behind made him look up in the mirror. Amira stood in the doorway—the light from behind making her clothing translucent and haloing her blond hair. He clenched his hands on the edge of the basin. She was beautiful—a pity that it only went skin deep. Knowing that made it easier to do what he had to eventually do. Women like Amira had to learn that with wealth, came privilege—and with privilege, responsibility to others less fortunate.

"If you've forgotten anything, there should be toiletries in the drawers and cupboard. Help yourself, won't you."

He watched as her fingers played with the knot of her blouse. Pleating the short tail of fabric over and over. A sure sign she was nervous. Help himself? He knew where he wanted to start. With her. Here. Now. He swallowed and turned to face her.

"I'm sure I'll be fine."

"Good, well, I'll go downstairs and put on the coffee. Turn left at the bottom of the stairs when you're ready to come down and then left again to the back of the house."

Brent hung up the two changes of clothing he'd brought for the weekend. It didn't take long; after all, they weren't here for a fashion shoot. Which begged the question, what exactly were they here for? There was a skittishness about Amira he couldn't quite put his finger on. He'd lay odds she didn't only want to discuss wedding arrangements.

He had no trouble finding the kitchen. All he'd needed to do when he got downstairs was follow the delicious aroma. Fresh waffles steamed on a plate in the center of a scarred pine table and coffee percolated noisily on the stove top.

"I wasn't sure how you liked your waffles," Amira said as she gestured for him to sit down at the table, "so there's cream, fresh fruit and syrup. Whatever takes your fancy, really."

There was enough food here to feed an army. As he loaded his plate Brent couldn't help feeling that she was in some way overcompensating—the question was, for what?

"What did you have planned for today? Shall we start with the guest list?" he said as he helped himself to a second cup of coffee.

"We've got plenty of time to get that finalized. I was thinking, while the weather's still good, how about we head to the beach? There's a Jet Ski in the boatshed. I can take you for a tour around this end of the island if you like, while our breakfast settles. Then maybe we can have a swim?"

"Sure, sounds like a plan." So already she was putting off finalizing the wedding arrangements. Interesting, considering it was the reason behind her insistence he come over to Windsong for the weekend.

They changed after breakfast. Amira into a bikini top and shorts, Brent into a T-shirt and swim trunks. He couldn't tear his eyes away from her tanned belly. It tantalized and teased, drawing his attention to the slenderness of her waist and the rounded curve of her hips, the cradle of her pelvis. It was all too easy to imagine her wearing nothing at all.

As they climbed on board the Jet Ski, Amira turned her head back to him.

"You might want to slide a bit closer to me and put your arms around my waist. It gets a bit choppy in the channel."

In any other circumstances he wouldn't have hesitated, but even the thought of sliding forward so his thighs cradled the soft roundness of her buttocks, had him already half-erect. His hesitation was almost his undoing as he slid back a bit on the seat when she opened up the throttle and headed out into the bay. Holding on to her was the only sensible option, but he'd be damned if he was going to pull himself hard up against her while he did so. He wanted to drive her crazy, not the other way around.

She was an excellent guide, pointing out several properties owned by various members of New Zealand's elite, as well as some areas of historical significance. As they headed back to their bay he even started to feel himself relax. Then, suddenly, somehow in their sweep into the bay and toward the boathouse he managed to end up ignominiously in the water. As he sputtered to the surface, the air rang with Amira's laughter.

"Wretch. You'll pay for that," Brent warned with a determined smile on his face as he struck out toward the Jet Ski.

She may have taken him by surprise this time, but she wouldn't get away with that again. He latched on to Amira's foot before she could maneuver away, and suddenly she was there, in his arms, her full breasts hard against his chest, her legs swirling in the water around his. His blood pressure instantly ratchetted up a notch, his breathing quickened. His arms tightened around her, his legs entwined with hers. She couldn't mistake the strength of his reaction to her.

His eyes locked with hers, and he saw something change in her expression. All humor died, to be replaced with something else. Something elemental—hungry. He stopped treading water, and they slowly began to slide beneath the surface. Instantly he let her go and felt her push toward the surface. As he kicked back up and broke the surface himself, he saw Amira pulling herself back up onto the Jet Ski.

"I—I'll put this away, okay? Did you want to come in now or stay in the water a bit longer?"

She didn't make eye contact, instead lifting her arms to wring out her hair. The movement made her breasts lift, exposing the underside of each lush globe beneath the bottom edge of her bikini bra. That did it. Brent ripped off his T-shirt and bunching it up into a ball, threw it toward her, where it landed on the running board with a slap.

"Take that in for me would you? I think I'll swim for a bit. Work off some of that breakfast." And not a little bit of the sexual frustration that held him in its grip.

With a nod she turned the Jet Ski and returned it to the boatshed. Brent couldn't help but watch her as she made her way back down the jetty, stopping only for a moment to slip off her wet shorts and carry them together with his T-shirt to the beach where she laid them over the branches of a nearby pohutukawa tree. Swim, he told himself. Swim hard.

Despite it being early April, the water temperature in the sea was still bearable. Brent swam the width of the cove with punishing strokes and then turned to swim back again. Eventually, he slowed his pace slightly and turned toward the beach, to where Amira lay on the lounger on the sand. She was watching him, he could feel it, and it did nothing to ease the ache building up inside of him. As he rose from the water he heard her laugh.

"You're supposed to be here to relax, not exhaust yourself." She smiled as she rose from the lounger and picked up his towel.

She sauntered over to him and shook out the towel. He went to take it, but she ignored him, instead, beginning to dry him herself. Trails of fire followed her touch as she dragged the terry cloth over his arms and then across his chest. His nipples contracted into tight beads as she stroked across his rib cage and then drew the towel lower, to his abdomen, his waist.

"Thanks," he said, grabbing the towel from her and turning slightly away so she couldn't see the havoc her touch had wreaked.

"No problem."

He could hear the amusement in her voice. Amusement blended with something else. He flicked a glance at her. Oh yes, it was definitely arousal. Beneath the white triangles of her bikini top her nipples were equally as hard as his own, and her chest rose and fell as if she was the one who'd just completed a marathon swim. What was going on? She'd been so cool and remote these past two weeks, and now it was as if she was a smoldering ember, ready to light up at any time.

Had their proximity been as difficult for her as it had been for him? Another thought occurred to him. Or was this her secret agenda? Did she plan to seduce him into going through with the wedding? Had that article rattled her Forsythe cool so much that she was willing to sully herself with him one more time?

As he balanced the idea in his head, his all-too-eager flesh reminded him of how her touch had ignited his desire. If seduction was her intention, he certainly didn't plan on putting any roadblocks in her way. Oh no. If anything, he wished she'd make her intentions clear so he could rid himself of some of this tension that had been building up since the day she'd cornered him in the chapel men's room.

Amira watched as Brent finished drying himself, threw his towel down on the sand and then himself facedown after it. Had she gone too far, drying him like that? She didn't want to scare him off. She smiled ruefully. Scare off someone like Brent Colby? Now there was the definition of impossible. But getting back to her goal, she had to be careful. She needed to woo him, to slowly seduce him, not to rush at him like a bull at a gate no matter what her hormones were begging her to do.

She stretched out languorously on the lounger and sighed. Who'd have thought this would be so difficult? It wasn't as if they were strangers to one another physically, and the past few weeks had proven they could work well together—paint a believable facade.

"That's the third time you've sighed in the past couple of minutes. What's up?" Brent interrupted her thoughts.

Amira forced a laugh. "I think I'm finding this relax and chill out time more difficult to get into than I thought," she covered quickly.

"Maybe you're trying too hard," Brent said as he rolled halfway over to face her. "We should probably head back to the house and get this wedding stuff out of the way. Then maybe you'll be able to relax."

"Yeah, I think you're right." Because God only knew she was struggling right now.

Just as she straightened to sit up in her chair and gather her things from beside her, a huge wet drop of rain landed smack between her shoulder blades. She squealed in shock.

"We'd better hurry," Brent said, leaping to his feet in one sensuous glide of man and muscle. "That cloud's about to burst."

He'd no sooner spoken than the cloud did just that, drenching them and their gear within seconds with pelting drops of rain. Brent bent and dragged his towel up off the wet sand and grabbed Amira's hand, tugging her back toward the house. Caught off balance she stumbled, landing heavily in the soft sand and pulling him after her.

"Look at us, full of sand. We'll need to go around the back." She laughed breathlessly as they got back up and scrambled across the beach, kicking up more sand as they went. "There's an outdoor shower near the pool. We can wash the sand off before we go inside."

"What about our stuff?"

"Hey, it's soaked now. A bit more water isn't going to hurt it. We can pick it up later."

They ran across the lawn, and she gestured to the right-hand side of the house.

"That way. There's cover."

They skittered to a halt just inside the portico that housed the outdoor shower. An intricate latticework of trellis between narrow pillars provided a measure of privacy from the poolside. Not that anyone was there to watch them.

"Here, you go first, I'll grab some fresh towels from the pool house," she said after reaching over and turning on the shower faucet.

She was back in a moment. She ducked under the roof and put the towels she'd collected on the shelves just inside the door. Outside, the rain continued to bucket down. She turned to face Brent and almost wished she'd waited outside in the rain until he was done.

He stood beneath the showerhead, his arms up against the wall above him, the long deep triangular shape of his shoulders and tapered muscled back bared for her scrutiny. His trunks clung to the outline of his backside—hugging the gentle curve of his butt cheeks. Rivulets of water ran over him, and she wished she had the courage to reach out and track their path as they wended their way down to his waistband.

"I— Ah, I've brought the towels."

"You want to get under the shower with me?"

Amira swallowed. Did she? Oh Lord, yes—more than anything. But would she be moving too fast again? Before she could overthink the situation, he put out his hand to her and she moved forward, sliding under the showerhead and letting the warm water pour over her scalp and through her hair. Brent filled his hand with soap from the soft soap dispenser on the wall and smoothed the slightly spice-scented liquid across her back and down to her waist before sliding around to the front and moving back up to her shoulders again.

She closed her eyes as the water ran over her face, but they flew open again just as quickly as Brent loosened the ties of her bikini bra.

"What are you doing?"

"You're bound to have sand stuck in there. You want to be comfortable when you dry yourself, don't you?"

Words failed her as his fingers completed their task, and her bikini top fell on the tiled floor beneath them.

Ten

"Amira, turn around."

His voice was low and deep, and without thought she slowly turned to face him. Her breath hitched again at the expression on his face.

"You always were too beautiful for words," he said softly, before reaching out a finger to trace the areola of one nipple with a featherlight caress.

Her skin tightened at his touch, an almost unbearable wave of need swamping through her body—wishing him to touch her again.

"Brent?"

The sound that escaped on his name was both a plea and a question. In answer he bent his dark head to her breast and caught her nipple between his lips. As he stroked his tongue around the hardened peak, her legs threatened to buckle. His strong arm slid around her waist, pulling her to him, holding her against that part of his body that left her in no doubt as to how much he wanted her right this minute. And, oh, did she want him. It felt so right to be in his arms, to feel the power of his muscles beneath her fingertips. They fit together as if they'd never been apart, her body clamoring for his touch, her mouth watering for the taste of him.

He transferred his attention to her other breast, his tongue darting over the surface, lapping at the water that ran over her skin, sending sensation spiraling through her body.

She had to touch him, feel him. She slid her fingers beneath the waistband of his trunks and eased them away, far enough so she could push her hands inside to caress the hot hard shaft of his passion for her. He flinched slightly at her touch, a low growl sounding deep in his throat.

He pulled away from her slightly, meeting her gaze with a heated stare.

"Are you sure you want to do this?"

"Ye—"

"Before you answer," he interrupted, placing his lips against hers and stealing her response before she could finish, "be very sure of what you're going to say, because if you say yes, I won't be able to stop."

A thrill of excitement rippled through her. Stop? Oh no, she didn't ever want him to stop.

"Yes," she whispered against his lips, flicking her

tongue across the seam of his mouth for emphasis. "Yes, I want this. Yes, I want you. Yes, I don't want you to stop."

Brent's body shuddered in response to her reply, and he took her lips with his in a kiss that was as fierce as it was mind-numbingly intense. He pressed her against the tiled wall of the shower and swiftly undid the side ties on her bikini. She parted her legs slightly to let the wet fabric fall away, to expose herself to him, to his touch.

His fingers danced over her curls, softly, gently. So gently she wanted to scream at him to take her. But then she felt his hand cup her and a shimmer of pleasure made her groan out loud.

"How long? How long since you've felt like this?" His hand shifted, his fingers parting her, stroking at the entrance to her inner heat.

"Forever." She could barely enunciate the word.

She hadn't been with another man since the last time she'd made love with Brent in the week before their aborted wedding. She knew no man could ever measure up to this. To him. Her legs quaked as he slowly slid one finger into her honeyed depths.

She didn't want to think. She only wanted to feel. And feel she did as he withdrew his finger to move a little higher, to circle the swollen bud of sensation that begged for his touch before sliding back inside her again. He'd always known exactly how to bring her pleasure. Exactly how to send her hurtling into a realm where sensation ruled.

"I want you inside me," she moaned, pressing herself hard against the palm of his hand.

He had her so close already, but she wanted him inside her when she came. Somehow she managed to push his wet trunks down over his hips. He kicked them away from his legs and then lifted her against the wall. She hooked her legs around his hips. She could feel his pulsing heat against the core of her, feel the hardness of him as he positioned himself at her entrance.

He hesitated, and she groaned in frustration.

"Protection," he muttered.

"It's okay. I've got it. I'm safe," she ground out as she uttered a silent prayer begging forgiveness for her lie.

And then he was inside her. Gloriously filling her, driving harder and faster until her inner muscles clenched against him, until he probed that special place that sent her mindlessly screaming over the edge. She felt him pump against her, once, twice more, then his hoarse cry told her he'd let go and joined her on the ephemeral cloud of pleasure and sensation that rippled through her again and again.

The low afternoon sun was trying to break through the clouds by the time Amira woke. She watched as Brent slept on. She smiled quietly to herself. After their time in the shower, they'd managed to make their way upstairs, amazing really when she considered how boneless he'd left her after that first time. And it had been the first of several as they rediscovered one another, sometimes slow and painstakingly gentle, other times fast and desperate, as they'd been in the pool shower.

Her heart swelled as she watched him—committing

each line of his face, the fall of his hair across his forehead, the sensual fullness of his lower lip, to her memory. Her hand lay across her belly. Had they done it? Had they begun the miracle process to create a child? She certainly hoped so, because once she told him they could no longer marry he'd be angry. So angry he might never want to see her or talk to her again. But if they'd made a baby, she'd have a special part of him forever.

She rolled over on the bed of the master suite and looked at the clock. Nearly five. No wonder she'd woken. She was starving. She slid from the bed and padded naked through the room to get a robe from her own wardrobe.

"Where are you going?" Brent raised a sleepy head from his pillow.

"Just to put something on and get something for us to eat."

"Don't."

"Don't get anything to eat?"

"No, don't put anything on."

Brent sat up and swung his legs off the side of the bed. He crossed to where she was standing in only a moment. He bent to kiss her, his hand possessively snaking around her waist and pulling her against him.

"I'll help you."

Laughter burbled from Amira's throat. "Help me? Distract me is more like it."

She spun out of his arms and flew down the carpeted hall and then swiftly ran down the stairs, Brent hard on her heels. He caught up with her in the kitchen, trapping her faced against the kitchen bench. She could feel his arousal against her buttocks. Despite herself she couldn't help but squirm against him.

"Distraction, did you say?" Brent said, his breath hot against the side of her neck.

She was helpless in his embrace—helpless to refuse what he promised with the slide of his tongue along the cord of her neck. When he gently kneed her legs farther apart and pulled her hips back to him to position himself to enter her once more, she gripped the kitchen countertop and fought back the moan of pleasure that built from deep inside.

How could she not have been driven mad missing this intensity between them? This insatiable need to be together, connected as one. As Brent's hands slid up over her hips and around to her belly, skimming the surface of her skin until they cupped her full breasts, his fingertips and thumbs teasing and pulling at her nipples, she acknowledged that she'd never stopped loving him and never would.

A shaft of heat speared through her body, from breast to deep in her belly. She pushed back against him, matching his rhythm, urging him on faster and harder until he groaned, his body pulsing deep inside her, and her climax spiraled out to claim her every sense, her every emotion.

Weak with satisfaction, she leaned forward on her arms, bracing herself against the counter. She'd never be able to enter this kitchen again without remembering this moment. Brent coaxed her body upright, turning her around to face him.

Brent battled to get his heart rate under control, reminding himself that while sex was one thing, his self-appointed task was quite another. It would be all too easy to allow his mind to be as seduced by their near-insatiable desire for one another as his body had been. He had to keep the upper hand—to remember what she'd done to him and what he'd vowed to make her pay for. He had to remember how carelessly she'd put the Fulfillment Foundation in jeopardy.

He reached out a hand and smoothed Amira's tumbled golden locks from her face, cupped her chin and lifted it to present her for his kiss.

"You okay? That was…" His voice petered off, lost for words to describe the overwhelming need he'd had to possess her.

He'd thought the edge would have worn off a little now; instead, each time, it only whet his appetite for more.

"Yeah, it was…" She smiled. "I'm fine. What about you? Hungry?"

He kissed her again. "Always, but some food would be a good idea too."

He leaned back against the bench as she went to the fridge and pulled out a plate of gourmet cheeses and placed it on a tray on a side counter. She added some sliced fruit she'd obviously also prepared earlier, as well as a loaf of French bread and some crackers. A small jar of relish completed the tray.

"There's some wine in the fridge and glasses in the cupboard over there. You take care of those, and I'll take the tray upstairs. This can tide us over until dinner later on."

"Sure," Brent replied, grabbing the bottle of chilled Marlborough grown and bottled chardonnay from the fridge door and snagging two wineglasses from the cupboard.

Later on sounded just fine to him, because it meant something else came before, he smiled to himself as he followed Amira back up the stairs to his room.

By the time the launch arrived to take them back to the city on Sunday they'd eventually gotten around to finalizing their guest lists for the wedding and all the minutiae that Amira insisted were important. More than once Brent had had to quell the pang that he was setting her up for major disaster. It was what he had set out to do all along, he reminded himself. One way or another, it was going to happen, and with it he'd remove her power to devastate others' lives along the way.

He was surprised to see Amira had arranged separate cars to take them back to their respective homes.

"You don't want to come back to my place?" he asked.

Amira ducked her head, not quite meeting his eyes when she answered. "I'm sorry, not tonight. I've got a really early start in the morning."

"Yeah, me too," Brent said. But still he had the sensation that she was hiding something. It irritated him that he couldn't put his finger on exactly what that was.

Across the street from the wharf, Brent espied a particularly persistent photographer who'd dogged their every step in the past few weeks.

"Look, he's here already." He nodded in the general

direction where the photographer lurked. "Let's give him the scoop he's been waiting for, hmm?"

With that he pulled Amira to him and wrapped her in his arms. Her lips softened beneath his, opening for the sweep of his tongue, all reticence gone under his touch. God, he couldn't get enough of the taste of her, of the velvet of her mouth. When he broke off the kiss, his blood pressure had gone up several points and his breathing was ragged.

"If I didn't have an early flight to Sydney in the morning I'd be finishing off on the promise of that kiss," he growled against her lips.

"I'll just look forward to when you come back then, shall I?" Amira patted his cheek and gave him a swift peck before turning to get into the waiting limousine that would take her home.

Brent stood a while longer, watching as she was driven away, still intensely aware of the imprint of her against his body. His return home wasn't all she had to look forward to, he told himself grimly as he handed his bag to the driver waiting to take him home.

Eleven

Amira watched the color change on the indicator stick of the home pregnancy test she'd bought. Her heart raced as she laid it next to the other three she'd already lined up on her bathroom vanity. She sank to the floor, her legs tucked under her, as the reality of the series of positives rammed home.

Pregnant. With Brent's child.

She laid her hand against her stomach as if she could already feel the differences taking place inside her. Tears rolled down her cheeks. She hadn't believed it could be so easy—that the time they'd spent together on the island at Windsong had so swiftly brought the results she'd wanted. At some time in that sinfully hedonistic weekend they'd hit the jackpot. She hadn't wanted to believe it had happened so quickly. She wouldn't even let herself begin to hope when she missed her first period after that weekend. It was only now, after missing her second period, she'd begun to dream it could be true.

In the past month she and Brent had spent a great deal of time together, forging what she believed had been a new closeness. A closeness that to her was all the more bittersweet because she knew it couldn't last, despite her wishes to the contrary. They'd dined together most nights, slept together most nights—spending time together just for the sheer joy of it.

And now she had to rip all that apart and tell him she wouldn't be marrying him in two weeks' time. The tears increased in frequency as a sob ripped from her throat. She should be happy—ecstatic, even—she reminded herself. Sometime before the end of December she'd be a mother, well before her thirtieth birthday as demanded by Isobel's will. Her dreams for the Fulfillment Foundation would be realized.

Even so, she felt so dreadfully empty inside. Bereft. How on earth was she going to summon the courage to tell Brent the news that their wedding was off? She was cutting it fine. Two weeks to the wedding. What if she'd had to stand him up again on the day? Her stomach pitched uncomfortably, making her draw in a steadying breath.

Slowly the tears dried, and a sense of calm began to settle on her shoulders. First things first, she had to get official medical confirmation of her pregnancy. She pulled herself to her feet and swept the test results and their packaging into the bathroom waste bin. It would be tricky getting an appointment with one of Auckland's leading obstetricians without having the media get a hold of the information and effectually blowing her secret into the stratosphere of gossip.

She looked in the mirror and lifted her chin. She wasn't a Forsythe for nothing. She'd pull whatever strings she could to ensure her privacy, even if it meant having everyone attend to her here at the house.

Amira sat at the table of the famed Okahu Bay seafood restaurant on Auckland's waterfront and looked back at the city. It was a perfect mid-autumn day. A light breeze ruffled the sea and a dozen small yachts engaged in trying to make the most of the wind as they jostled about in the bay and beneath the sea wall. Across the road from the restaurant a school group of kayakers made a colorful splash against the blue of the water. In the distance, the towers of Auckland City punctuated the intense blue skyline.

She sighed. A perfect day to be doing the least perfect thing she'd ever had to undertake in her life. Today she was going to tell Brent the wedding was off—face-to-face. No text message this time. She'd deliberately chosen this public setting because she knew Brent wouldn't make a scene here. Not that he'd make a scene exactly anywhere else, but she knew she'd need the buffer of other people around her to at least keep the exchange on a civil level.

The hair on the back of her neck prickled. He was here. She turned and smiled as he walked toward her, immaculate in his black perfectly-cut suit, an open-necked turquoise, black-and-white-striped shirt beneath it. His eyes were hidden by the dark-lensed designer sunglasses he wore, but she could see he was pleased to see her. His lips curved into an answering smile as he bent to give her a kiss.

As brief as it was, she felt it all the way to her toes, and she hoarded the sensation to her. It was the last time they'd be so intimate. She thought of the life growing within her. At least she'd have that, she reminded herself.

"Have you chosen what you want to eat yet?" Brent asked as he lowered himself into his chair adjacent to hers and picked up the wine menu.

"Not yet. I thought I'd wait for you."

"I'm easy. I'll have the seafood medley. Why don't you try the scallops. I hear they're delicious."

When she nodded her assent he gestured to the waiter, placed their order and pointed to the award-winning Pinot Gris on the wine list that had recently become his favorite.

"Oh, no wine for me, thanks. I'll just stick with mineral water today," Amira interrupted as Brent started to order a bottle of the wine.

"You're sure? Well, in that case, just bring me a glass for now," Brent told the waiter. He turned his gaze back on Amira. "Are you feeling okay? You're a bit pale."

"I'm fine, really. Just a little tired is all." Amira rushed over the words.

She hadn't realized the strain of what she was going

to do was showing a physical effect already. They made desultory conversation until their main courses arrived. Amira could barely eat the delicately flavored seared scallops drizzlcd with a lime and coconut cream dressing. Instead, she slid them one by one off their skewers and pushed them about her plate. She jumped when Brent reached out and put his hand on hers.

"What's up? Something's bothering you."

Her stomach flip-flopped uncomfortably, and the words she needed to say clogged in her throat. Tears burned at the back of her eyes as she raised her gaze from her plate to meet his. There was no avoiding it. She had to tell him.

"I'm calling off the wedding. I can't go through with it."

There, she'd said it. She reached for her mineral water and took a sip, surprised to see her hand so steady as she put the glass back on the table.

"You what?" Brent's voice was deadly cold, but the heated slashes of color that appeared on his cheeks gave immediate insight to his anger.

His hazel eyes narrowed as he met her gaze, reminding her of the predatory stare in a panther's eyes before it struck its prey. Amira fought back the tremor that threatened to rock through her body and focused on her breathing, on calming the now erratic beat of her heart.

"I've asked Marie to prepare a statement to the media to say that we've both agreed to withdraw from our engagement."

Rage flared inside him, hot and fast, threatening to

consume the cool demeanor that was his trademark in
business. Brent beat back the flames of fury before they
could erupt. How the hell long had she been planning
this? He chose his next words carefully fighting to keep
his voice level.

"You talked to Marie about this before you told me?"

"I had to."

"You had to," he repeated. He lifted his glass and took
a long sip of his wine. "And what made you decide you
had to break our engagement? Hmm? Last I saw, my finances were still intact. Had a better offer, perhaps?"

He saw her flinch at his words and allowed a slither
of satisfaction to slide beneath his anger. His vengeance
was slipping through his fingers, and he was helpless to
stop it. He didn't do helpless.

"Your financial position has nothing to do with it,
Brent. Look, can we be civil about this, please?"

"Civil? You want me to be civil? How about a reason
why, Amira? Wasn't last night good enough for you?"
He leaned forward and pitched his voice low so only she
could hear him. "Didn't you come apart in my arms as
we made love, as I kissed your body? All over."

To his satisfaction, a flush rose in her cheeks and a
tiny gasp broke from her lips. Lips that had in return
touched him in places that warmed and roused to her
touch with an alacrity that left him raging with a heated
desire that showed no sign of abating. Not even now.

"I thought I could deal with it, go through with the
wedding but I can't." She picked up the white linen
napkin from her lap and dabbed at her lips, her knuckles

gleaming white as she clutched the stiff white cloth. "It's over, Brent. Please don't make this harder than it has to be."

She slid her engagement ring off and put it on the table between them. He leaned back in his chair and eyed her carefully. She refused to meet his gaze.

"Harder than it has to be. That's a joke. And what about the money you owe me. I agreed to your terms. We signed a contract. If you don't fulfil the terms of that contract, cent for cent, I will sue you for breach of promise—and won't that make for some interesting publicity?"

He may not have the satisfaction of doing to her what she had done to him eight years ago, but he drew some comfort that his demand she fulfill the terms of their contract would destroy her financially.

"I'm a woman of my word."

He scoffed in disbelief. "Really? Then what do you call this?"

Amira rose from her chair, dropped the cloth napkin onto her seat and gathered up her handbag. If he'd thought she was pale before, she was even paler now. A pang of sympathy was swiftly quashed. Let her be rattled by his demand. She'd learn soon enough that she couldn't wriggle out of the contract. That every last word was binding.

"I fulfilled the first part of our deal. You have the consents you needed, and you will get your money. I personally guarantee it."

With that she spun on her heel and headed for the

stairs leading out of the restaurant. From his position on the balcony table he watched as she walked with clipped steps to where her BMW was parked and gracefully got in then drove smoothly away. Without so much as a sign of any distress. Had she planned this all along? If so, he'd seriously underestimated her.

Brent played her parting words through his head. *You will get your money. I personally guarantee it.* How on earth was she going to do that? He knew for a fact she had no personal wealth of her own. No hidden offshore accounts that could possibly meet the multimillion dollar requirements of their agreement. She was in no position to *personally* guarantee anything.

So what, then, was she up to?

Amira drove toward the city, her hands clenched tight on the steering wheel. She'd done it. She'd actually done it and walked away. She should be feeling a sense of lightness, of relief. Instead she wanted to howl in misery. For the second time in her life, she'd rejected the man she loved above all others. For the second time because of her grandmother's control.

"You won't have any control over me anymore, Grandmother. This is the last time you pull my strings," she vowed through a throat choked with emotion.

She swung into the underground parking lot in the building housing her lawyer's offices and parked in the designated visitor's parking space. For a few moments she just sat there in the artificially illuminated glare, forcing her breathing to settle and her body to stop trembling. The journey from the restaurant to here had passed in a blur; she had no memory of the road she'd traveled. The knowledge frightened her. She couldn't afford to be so oblivious again, she scolded herself. She had another person to consider now, and she couldn't afford to put that tiny life at risk by any means.

The ride in the lift to the eighth floor was swift. A quick glance at the mirrored walls of the car confirmed she still looked the same as she had when she'd left home this morning. Still as cool and poised as if she hadn't just ripped her heart and her dreams into shreds. At least she had her training and poise to thank Isobel for, she admitted with a self-deprecating shake of her head. If nothing else.

She was ushered into Gerald Stein's office by one of his administrative staff as soon as she arrived in the main office. Gerald rose from his seat and put his hands on her shoulders, dropping a kiss on her forehead in welcome.

"My dear. How are you?"

She couldn't exactly tell him she was a total wreck, now could she?

"I've ended my engagement to Brent Colby and," she said while reaching into her handbag for the letter from her obstetrician, "I think you'll find that this confirms that I will still be able to meet the terms of Grand-mother's will."

She sat in a chair and watched as Gerald read the letter, his face changing from his usual calm demeanor to one of complete disbelief.

"You're pregnant?"

"Yes."

Gerald was speechless as he sat back down in his chair, shaking his head in denial.

"I can't believe you've done this."

"The terms of Grandmother's will were clear, were they not? Either marry before my thirtieth birthday or bear live issue before that date. Gerald, I'm not prepared to marry just any man to satisfy her dictates. No matter what hold she has over me I cannot do that. Nor can I just let my rightful inheritance slip into Roland's hands. You and I both know he'll burn through the immediately accessible funds before starting to sell off the other assets. A man like him would do irreparable damage, and then where would Grandmother's charities be?" Not to mention the Fulfillment Foundation, she added silently. "At least this way I'm not bound to someone I neither like nor respect, and I can still continue my charity work in Grandmother's stead. That *is* what she wanted, isn't it?"

"Well, yes, of course. But Amira, having a baby on your own is no small task. Are you sure you're doing the right thing? And what about the father? Who is he?"

"The baby's father is of no consequence." Sharp pain dragged through her chest. Of no consequence? He was everything but. Amira continued, "Besides, Grandmother left me no other option, did she?"

Amira reached into her handbag again and drew out her copy of the agreement she'd signed with Brent. She put it on the desk between them.

"Now, based on the fact that I am pregnant and can

fulfill her stipulations, I want you to raise a loan for that sum." She stabbed her forefinger at the amount written in words and in figures in the middle of the agreement. "And I want you to pay that to Brent Colby."

"What? You can't be serious. Amira, that's an enormous sum of money. It's not as if Colby needs it."

"Whether he needs it or not, it's what we agreed to when we became engaged. I'm still obligated to keep up my end of the deal." Amira tried to ignore the stab of pain in the region of her heart. Oh, how she wished it could have been different.

"Surely there's a loophole or an escape clause." Gerald slid his glasses down his nose and peered at her, realization dawning on his wrinkled face. "Oh no, Amira. Tell me you didn't sign this without a legal opinion."

"I read the document thoroughly. It encapsulated everything we'd agreed upon. There are no loopholes. Gerald, I was quite happy to marry Brent until you disclosed that additional clause. Had I known about that from the beginning...well, things obviously would have taken a different path, wouldn't they?"

"But Amira, this agreement says nothing about not having to meet your obligations if the wedding doesn't take place." Gerald read aloud the clause that looked like it was on the verge of triggering a coronary. "*And furthermore, the said Amira Camille Forsythe will make over to the said Brent Colby a sum of money being not less than ten percent of the amount Amira Camille Forsythe would inherit upon the occasion of her marriage.* Would inherit! This is disastrous!"

Gerald placed the paper on his desk and rubbed at his chin before continuing. "This has been so broadly phrased that it wouldn't have mattered who you married or even *if* you married. Amira, you are obligated to pay this money to Colby no matter what happens."

Gerald's words died on the air as the truth behind them slowly sank in. Brent had set her up all along. Whether she went through with their marriage or not, he'd stood to gain massively. Amira reached her decision quickly. No matter what Brent's motives, hers had been less than honest also. She'd promised to pay him, and now she could afford to. In every transaction there was always collateral damage to some degree. She could put this behind her now and move on.

"Gerald, you're my lawyer. Grandmother's estate pays you to take instructions from me unless I fail to meet the terms of my inheritance. Is that correct?" Amira fought to hold on to the final shred of control she had left.

"That's correct, of course. But I'm more than that, my dear, and you know it," Gerald said.

"Then, please, in this instance, can we keep emotion out of the equation. I'd like you to raise a loan for the money I promised to make available to Brent, and I'd like you to see to it that he receives that money as quickly as possible. Please defer repayment of the loan until two weeks after the due date of my baby."

"If that is your last word on the matter—"

"It is. I'm sorry to have to be so blunt, Gerald, but you know I have no other choice."

Choice, as she understood the term, had never been

hers. But, she thought as she pressed her hand against her belly, that would change with the advent of this new life, this new hope for her future.

Twelve

"There's how much been deposited?" Brent fought not to shout down the receiver at his bank manager.

The man repeated the sum. Brent thanked him then replaced the phone. How on earth had she raised that much money in less than a fortnight? Tomorrow would have been their wedding day, the day he'd been looking forward to as his *coup de grâce* in their relationship. The day where he'd finally extract his revenge. But she'd forestalled him in that quest, and now, it appeared, she'd preempted his attempt to drive her into financial ruin.

Something wasn't right. He paced to the window of his home office and gazed out across the estuary. She should be destitute and frantic, not calmly depositing several million dollars in his bank account.

There had to be more to her grandmother's will than she'd let on. Some other clause that had given her a different method of accessing the funds she so desperately needed. But what was that clause?

Brent spun back to his desk and punched in a series of numbers on his phone before switching it to speaker. When his investigator answered, he wasted no time in getting to the point.

"I need to see a copy of Isobel Forsythe's will. What will it take?"

"It's simple enough. A letter of application to the High Court together with payment of their fee and it's yours."

"Then what are you waiting for?"

"I'll apply to the registrar, Mr. Colby, but it may take some time."

"I don't pay you to keep me waiting."

"Yes, sir. When do you want it?"

"Yesterday," Brent barked at the phone before disconnecting the call.

He raked his hands through his hair, then clasped his fingers behind his head and stretched against the tautness in his neck and shoulders. What the hell had Amira been up to?

Later that afternoon an e-mail arrived with a scanned copy of the late Isobel Forsythe's will as an attachment. Brent glanced over the basics—the bequests to staff and to charities—finally he reached the part he'd been looking for.

He felt all the blood drain from his face as he read the subclause under the conditions of Amira's entitlement to inherit that stated in cold black and white that she was never to marry him under any circumstances. There'd never been any love lost between the old battle-ax and Brent, but this? This was proof the woman was nothing more than a manipulative monster. How dare she have toyed with Amira's life—her happiness—like that.

It made more sense about why Amira had canceled their plans and withdrawn from their arrangement. He didn't want to feel any pity or sympathy for her, but this gross influence over her life was unbelievable. He'd long believed that Isobel had kept Amira under her thumb for her own purposes, much like a personalized marionette, there to do her bidding. This was proof positive of his theory.

Another thought occurred to him. How long had Amira known about this? Surely she'd seen a full copy of the will. Surely she'd known even before she asked him to marry her that she couldn't do that and inherit at the same time. What the hell had she been up to?

There was more. Brent read on, and his earlier disgust was rapidly replaced with a new level of fury he'd never believed himself capable of.

Live issue. The two words swam before his eyes.

Damn her to hell and back. She'd cold-bloodedly allowed him to think he'd seduced her all so she could have a baby to access her inheritance. She'd played the ice maiden, being so inaccessible as to drive him to distraction and insisting on their arrangement being strictly business when all along she'd planned to have his child.

He clenched his hands in an attempt to control the

urge to pick up the top of the range laptop on his desk and hurl it through the nearest window. Oh, she was her grandmother's successor all right. He doubted even Isobel would have accepted a man in her bed for the sole purpose of procreation for financial gain.

A baby. *His* baby.

An overwhelming flood of emotion swamped him. A sense of connection to his as yet unborn son or daughter. No matter what Amira did, he'd make sure she didn't retain custody of the child once it was born. There was no way on this earth that Isobel's influence, through her scheming granddaughter, would taint his child.

He pushed his hands through his hair again and swore a blue streak. Amira would be sorry she'd ever deceived him. Sorry she ever thought to tangle with Brent Colby again. Oh, she'd pay for her deception. She'd pay dearly.

He picked up his phone again and punched in Amira's cell phone number only to hear the beeps that told him the number had been disconnected. He tried her home only to get the same.

He'd track her down eventually. She could run, but she couldn't hide from him forever.

The wind whipped around the headland, making the palms bordering Windsong sway and dance with a massive rustle of noise. Amira got up from the desk in the office she'd made her own since she'd left Auckland in an attempt to dodge the media circus that had erupted when the wedding had been canceled. The carefully worded request for privacy as they went their own ways was as casually discarded by the media as a day-old cup of coffee.

Two weeks after the announcement it had become impossible for her to stay in Remuera. Daily encampments of paparazzi made leaving the property a risk as her car was swamped and then chased by various means of transport. It had only been after she'd encountered a near miss with a photographer dangerously perched on the back of a motorcycle that she realized staying in her family home was putting both her and the baby at risk.

She'd made arrangements to be transported from the property in the dead of night in a removal van, which then took her to Mechanics Bay, from where a chartered helicopter had deposited her at the island.

For the past month that's exactly where she'd stayed—her only physical contact with other people being the small staff who maintained the property and the interior of the house. It was a lonely existence but a necessary one. No one had thought to see if she was here, instead fictional sightings of her in Sydney, Paris and London had effectively put everyone off the track.

She wondered what Brent thought. If he'd tried to contact her once he'd received the money. She missed him with an ache that went soul deep. Worse than the last time. She'd tried to keep busy, had submerged herself in the administrative duties she could manage to do with the Fulfillment Foundation and in the joys of discovering the week by week progress in her pregnancy.

Already she displayed the tiniest of baby bumps, and the other day, even though from her books she knew it was unlikely, she'd been certain the flutter she'd felt had been the baby's movement. Oh, how she wished she could have shared her excitement with Brent. But he could never know about the baby. She reminded herself again of the wording of the agreement—how he'd set her up to take her money, come hell or high water, no matter how much he said he didn't need it. If he knew about the baby no doubt he'd take steps to take it away from her too. She couldn't bear for that to happen. This was her child. Someone to call her own. Someone to love and who would love her unreservedly in return.

Tears flooded Amira's eyes, as they did so easily these days, spilling over her lashes and down her cheeks. She dabbed them away with one hand and focussed on the letter she had to e-mail back to her office in the city.

With the electronic and satellite setup Isobel had insisted on at Windsong, Amira had maintained contact with her staff at the Fulfillment Foundation. She swore them to privacy on the promise of a massive bonus provided no news of her whereabouts leaked out. So far so good.

Until yesterday morning.

She'd woken with a niggling ache low in her belly. After going to the toilet, she had been horrified to see a small amount of blood. Terror had torn through her. At fourteen weeks pregnant she'd thought she was past the worst of the danger time when it was most likely to lose a baby. She was well aware of the statistics, that as many as one in four pregnancies ended unexpectedly before the twenty week mark, but she'd been so well. Felt so safe.

Now, however, she was terrified. She'd gone straight back to her bed and called her obstetrician's office. The nurse she'd spoken to had been comforting, consoling her that the symptoms she'd experienced may well settle down, but she'd advised Amira to make her way to the specialist's rooms as soon as she could so they could do a scan and ensure that everything was as it should be.

Amira's next call had been to the helicopter company that had flown her out here. But due to the very high winds, it was impossible to get a chopper safely out to Windsong. Likewise, the swells that were running on the sea effectively trapped her where she was. Her island paradise, her sanctuary from the public eye, had turned into her worst nightmare.

She'd stayed in bed all day, and this morning, thank goodness, the weather had died down sufficiently for a chopper to be sent to bring her back to Auckland City.

She e-mailed the letter back to her assistant and shut down her computer. Then she grabbed her things. It was time to go out to the helipad at the back of the house and wait.

Her timing was impeccable. Just as she secured the back door, a sleek black helicopter came in over the ridge and hovered prior to setting down on the marked H on the expansive back lawn. Strange, she didn't recognize the logo on the side. It certainly wasn't the company she'd used to arrange her flight back to the city.

A tall dark form alighted from the helicopter. Sudden recognition dawned, and it was as if a shower of icy water had been dumped over her head. Brent. He'd found her.

He covered the distance between them in a few short strides, his jacket fluttering in the buffet of wind from the slowing rotor blades. There was no doubt at all that he was angry—very, very angry. With nowhere to run—or to hide—Amira stood her ground and fought back the rising nausea that suddenly surfaced.

"Amira. Running away again, I see?" He gestured to the small overnight bag the nurse had recommended she bring with her in case she needed to be admitted to their private hospital overnight.

"What business is it of yours where I am?" she replied with a snap in her voice she managed to dredge from deep inside. "I don't answer to you."

"Really?"

"Yes, really. Now, get off my property," she ordered in an attempt to channel her late grandmother's hauteur.

"Ah, but it's not your property yet. Is it?" he countered.

A wave of dizziness hit her, and she swayed slightly, battling to keep her balance. The sensation receded, leaving her feeling sick. Scared.

"Either way, you have no place here. Please, leave." To her disgust her voice wavered.

"We have things to discuss."

"We have nothing to discuss. I met my obligations to you under the terms of our agreement. You have your consents. You have your money. Now go."

The ache in her belly sharpened, and the bitter taste of fear flooded her mouth. How far away was her ride? She had to get to the specialist. She just knew it.

"But what about my baby?"

He knew? The realization slammed into her with the full impact of a freight train. The breath rushed from her lungs; spots danced before her eyes. Brent took a step toward her, his dark eyebrows drawn in a straight line across eyes that demanded answers.

"Were you planning to pay me for that too?" He said the words so casually, any bystander could be forgiven for thinking he was joking, until they saw the glare of intent in his gaze.

"That's ridiculous. I'm not pregnant. How could I be? Besides, I don't have time for a baby. I'm far too busy." Amira took a step back and rattled off her denial hoping he'd believe her.

All she wanted was to create space between them, but he was closing that space, stepping in until he was close enough that she could see the flecks of color in his eyes, smell the hint of cologne he wore, feel the heat emanating off his body in waves.

"Don't lie to me, Amira. I know the full conditions of Isobel's will. I know you used me and then discarded me like last year's fashion. Besides, you forget, I know you. *Intimately.* I can see the changes in you, even feel them."

He put his hand on the small swelling of her belly, the heat of his hand imprinting through the fabric of her winter dress, all the way to her skin. There it was again, that flutter, followed by another spear of pain.

"You don't know me at all. And, besides, you set me up all along. You didn't mean to go through with the wedding either, did you?"

His lips firmed into a straight line as he maintained a silence that told her more than any words.

"Just go. Leave me!" Amira cried on a sob.

He removed his hand and stepped back. "This doesn't end here. I will fight you with every last breath before I'll allow you to keep my child."

On that note, he turned and began to walk away. Amira raised a hand toward him in a silent plea as the dizziness returned again, as the pain increased.

"Brent?"

He turned at the sound of her voice. Something wasn't right. She was more than angry, more than defensive. She was frightened. And suddenly, so was he. She swayed, her eyelids fluttering. He closed the short distance between them in a flash, only to catch her in his arms as she lost consciousness. Gently he lowered her to the path, and cushioning her body against his own he checked her pulse, her breathing. As he did so he noticed the blood, and fear as he'd never known it before plunged through to his heart.

By now the chopper pilot was running toward him, with a first aid kit in hand. But this was more than any first aid kit could handle. Brent knew it.

"Call the rescue helicopter. Now!"

Brent smoothed her hair from her face and held her to him, desperate to impart his health and vitality back into her. He'd never before prayed in his life, but suddenly he was prepared to barter anything to keep safe the small life he knew was at risk before it was too late.

Thirteen

Amira looked around her hospital room and fought to swallow the sorrow that threatened to choke her. She could no longer hold on to any hope that her dreams for the future would come to fruition. She'd lost it all. Her inheritance, the Fulfillment Foundation, the man she loved and above all else, her baby.

And it was all her fault.

Oh sure, the specialist had said even if she'd made it the day before she'd collapsed there was nothing that could have been done. That some pregnancies are simply not to be. But deep down inside she knew she could never forgive herself.

She'd refused all visitors except Gerald. The colorful arrangements that had been delivered on a daily basis were an assault on eyes that had shed too many tears already, and she'd turned each display away, asking the nurses to move them to another room, another ward, anywhere people would appreciate them more than she.

She stood and walked to the window, oblivious to the leaden skies and the clouds that skidded along, pushed by powerful gusts of wind. She was still a bit shaky on her legs. The hemorrhage that had taken her baby had almost taken her life. Sometimes she almost wished it had, because what was left for her now?

The clouds burst open, the sudden downpour drenching all and sundry. Beneath the hospital, on the pathways, people scurried for cover. As she watched them, Amira had never felt more apart from the world than now.

"Are you ready to go, my dear?"

Gerald's voice stirred her into movement. He sounded as if he'd aged a thousand years in the past few days. Goodness knew she felt as if she had too.

"Yes, I'm ready."

"Are you sure you want to go to the mansion? There's been all sorts of speculation in the media about why you were admitted to hospital. Some have even hinted at miscarriage. They won't leave you alone."

Amira flinched then forced herself to relax her shoulders and speak in level tone. "Let them speculate. Before long I'll be old news."

She started toward the door but Gerald stopped her, gesturing to a lone card on her bedside table.

"Don't you want to take that with you?"

Amira looked across the room at the colorful handmade

card little Casey McLauchlan had sent when the news had broken of her hospitalization. Gerald took it off the cabinet and handed it to her, but Amira shook her head.

"No, please leave it."

"But isn't it from one of the children—?" Gerald gently laid it facedown on the bed. "Ah, I see."

But he didn't see. He'd never understand how devastating it had been to receive that message of cheer from a child she'd promised the earth and then let down. She'd failed in this as she'd failed in everything. Her grandmother had been right all along.

After Gerald had settled her back in at her apartment, he sat down in the chair next to the sofa where she'd flopped on entering.

"I hate to bring this up now, Amira, but there's something we really must discuss."

"I know. The loan. I can't think about that right now. Please, can you defer the finance company a few more days?"

"I'll see what I can do, but I have to warn you that they are pressing me for a response."

"Gerald, please?"

He patted her leg. "I know, my dear. I know. Now, if you're sure there's nothing more I can do for you right now?"

"No. There's nothing. Thank you for bringing me back, and thanks for arranging the meals in the fridge. I don't think I'll be up to going anywhere for a few days at least."

"Of course not," he answered, patting her hand absently. "I'll see myself out. Don't hesitate to call if you need anything."

Amira smiled in response. She wouldn't be calling him. What she needed he simply couldn't provide. No matter how things went in the months leading up to her birthday, she knew she'd never meet Isobel's terms. She couldn't bear to put herself through the fear and worry of another pregnancy just to fulfill her grandmother's requirements; nor did she want to marry any man. The future stretched out in bleak silence ahead of her, the weight of worry about repaying the loan heavy on her mind.

As day turned to dusk, then night, she remained where she was. Eventually she roused herself from her stupor and went to the kitchen to make a cup of tea. As she passed her phone, she noticed the red light flashing on her message service. She pressed the button and gagged as Roland's voice filled the air.

"So sorry to hear about your miscarriage, darling. But never mind, if you play *nice,* I might still let you live with me. I've always fantasised about you. Would you like to hear it? Let me tell—"

Before he could complete his poisonous suggestion, Amira ripped the machine from its socket and threw it across the room with a cry of raw pain. Shaking, she slid down the wall, collapsing at the bottom. What on earth was she going to do?

The next day Amira roused herself into making an appearance at the foundation's offices. Anyone looking at her in her immaculately tailored dress, stockings and high-heeled boots would never imagine the turmoil that churned inside.

As she pushed open the front door to the office, she drew in a leveling breath, squared her shoulders and mentally rehearsed how she was going to tell her staff that it would probably be a good time for them to start looking for new jobs. Then, that done, she'd have to find the strength to personally contact each family on their register and apologize for failing them.

"Amira! I'm so glad you're here. I've been trying to call you all morning."

Caroline, her assistant, came racing through the main office, her face alight.

"You're never going to believe this. I didn't at first myself. But it's just wonderful, wonderful news!" Caroline bubbled with joy, her eyes gleaming and her face wreathed in a massive smile.

"Believe what," Amira asked. "Tell me. What's happened?"

Caroline's exuberance was infectious, and for a second, Amira could forget her grief as the beginnings of an answering smile began to pull at her lips.

"Come to my computer and see for yourself," Caroline said, taking Amira by the arm and tugging her past the other staff who all wore similar smiles and exuded the same air of suppressed excitement. "Here, sit down."

Caroline pushed her into her chair and pointed to her computer screen.

"There. See?"

Amira stared at the screen. Caroline was logged onto their Internet banking facility, their operating account's dismal record open for her to see. But what was that? Amira blinked to clear her eyes and looked again. That wasn't right. The sum in the account was massive. Seven figures massive. Her scalp prickled as she realized what this meant. The foundation could go on—for a while longer at least. But surely it was a mistake. The bank must have messed up somewhere along the line.

"Have you—?"

"Checked with the bank? Yes. They said the money was authorized by a benefactor who wished to remain anonymous."

An anonymous donor. Amira slumped in her seat. Could she dare to believe it was true? That finally her campaigning and soliciting for funds had borne fruit. Forget fruit; this was a whole orchard.

"That's amazing," she said weakly.

She got to her feet to face her staff, the people who she had thought only minutes ago she'd have to turn away. Beside her, Caroline began to clap and one by one each of the Fulfillment Foundation team rose to their feet and joined her in a standing ovation.

Tears gathered in Amira's eyes then overflowed down her cheeks—happy tears this time—and the ache in her heart began to ease a little. She might not have foreseen this solution to the foundation's financial woes, but she sure as heck wasn't going to look a gift horse in the mouth.

"Come on, everyone," she finally managed to say through her tears. "We have work to do!"

As everyone cheered then returned to their desks, Caroline threw her arms around Amira in a massive hug.

"You did it. I'm sorry I didn't believe you would," she whispered. "I'm so proud of you and of what we're doing here."

"Me too," Amira answered, lost in the comfort of her assistant's embrace. "Me too."

Amira settled at her desk and started to sort through the unopened mail that awaited her arrival. One in particular caught her eye. Marked "personal and confidential," it bore the logo of one of the inner-city law firms. Curious, she plucked it open and slid out the single sheet of paper inside. She scanned the words, first telling her about the anonymous donor and his generosity. Her eyes flicked back to the date of the letter. It was from before her time in the hospital. No wonder the sum in the bank had come as such a surprise to her staff. None of them would have opened her personal mail.

The small smile on her face froze as she continued to read the letter and read the next sentence. *This donation is being made under the condition that Amira Forsythe withdraw and step down from her association with the Fulfillment Foundation effective from the date of deposit of funds.* There were other sentences, but the words all ran together before her eyes.

Ice ran through her veins. Step down? Immediately? She didn't think anything could hurt her any more than she was hurt already, but this, the foundation, was all she had left. But the letter was clear. If she stayed, all financial assistance would be rescinded; if she left, the foundation would be assured of a regular influx of funds to ensure it continued its mission in the community.

Amira pushed her chair out from her desk and stood on shaking legs. All she had to do was countersign the bottom of the letter and fax it back to the firm in acceptance. Her hand dragged a pen across the page, and she went through the motions to ensure the fax went through.

She managed to get through the rest of the day encased in a state of numbness. Not even Casey's excited voice when informed of the details of her family's dream-come-true trip penetrated the frozen shell. By the end of the day, she was the last to leave the office. She put the letter she'd faxed to the anonymous donor's lawyers on Caroline's desk. Tomorrow would be soon enough for them all to know.

For the last time she wandered through the office, turned off the lights and locked the front door, pushing her key through the slot to fall silently to the carpet mat inside the door.

By the time she arrived back home, Amira couldn't care less that she bore little resemblance to the perfectly coiffed fashion plate who had left in the morning. Her hair was more out than in its twist, her lipstick had long ago worn off on the rims of countless cups of tea and her mascara lay in smudges under her eyes. Nothing mattered anymore.

She dragged her feet up the few steps to her private entrance and inserted her key in the front door. As she turned her key in the lock, it occurred to her that she was completely and truly alone. Alone and bankrupt. For the briefest time today she'd realized that her annuity wouldn't be needed to fund the foundation, but there was still the loan she had to repay.

Her annuity would barely touch the surface of the sum she had to repay, and all hope she'd nurtured of a future, died. Whatever money she had and whatever money she could potentially earn would be tied up for a very long time.

But at least the foundation would go on. She had to hold on to that dream. So what if it wouldn't be her dream anymore—she'd made it happen. She'd brought it to life.

Inside the house she forced herself into the shower in an attempt to warm her body. Afterward she changed into a fleece sweatshirt and track pants and sat down with yet another mug of tea, a notepad and pen. It was time to start seriously planning how she was going to manage—survive was more to the point. But nothing would come, and her paper remained blank. Eventually Amira picked up her mug and went through to the main house.

The furnishings shrouded in dust cloths had never been more eerie. She'd tried to make a habit of walking through the house at least once every couple of weeks to check that everything remained secure, but it had been a whole lot longer than that since she'd done so.

Ignoring the bottom floor, Amira trailed up the staircase, stopping to toast her grandmother briefly on the way up.

"You win again, Grandmother. I hope you're happy, wherever you are."

She took a sip of her tea and wondered anew at what had driven Isobel to be so harsh toward her only grand-daughter. Whatever it had been, Amira had no way of ever knowing. She carried on up to where her father's portrait hung and sank to the floor, desperate for some sense of connection to the handsome smiling man whose eyes were so much like her own.

How different would things have been, she wondered, if he and her mother hadn't died that day? She shook her head. She could no more change the past than she could satisfy Isobel's posthumous demands.

She searched her memory for the sound of her father's voice, the feel of his arms around her, but some-where in the last eighteen years she'd lost all that. All that and so very much more. Yet, on the periphery of her mind lingered the sensation of being loved, of being happy. She wanted that again; oh how she wanted to feel like that again.

"Amira?"

She knocked over her mug on the carpet runner as she struggled to rise on feet that stung with pins and needles from the way she'd been sitting.

"Brent? What on earth—?"

She drank in the sight of him. Dressed in faded jeans and a heavy black woollen sweater, he was a feast for her eyes. But she had to remember his betrayal, his anger. Amira forced herself to clamp down on the surge of emotion rocketing through her.

"You didn't answer your front door—it was unlocked so I let myself in. I was worried about you. You wouldn't see me at the hospital. I had to see for myself that you were okay."

She drew herself up to her full height and met his gaze, summoning every shred of Forsythe sangfroid at her fingertips.

"Well, you needn't have worried. As you can see, I'm fine." *Please leave now, before I break down again.*

"I…I wanted to say I was wrong and," he said and sighed deeply, "I'm sorry."

Sorry? The word tore the breath from her throat, making it impossible to speak. He shifted under her incredulous stare, as if for once in his life he wasn't the strong and confident man she knew him to be. As she watched him, he made as if to speak again, then shook his head slightly and turned to go back down the stairs.

"Wait!" she cried out, anger blooming in her chest where before only pain had resided.

Brent stopped on the stairs.

"You can't just say you're sorry and then leave. So you're sorry. So what? Why? You made it perfectly clear what you thought of me. You even planned to set me up for failure. Is that what you're sorry about? Because if that's all it is, you can take your apology and you can sho—!"

Brent ascended the stairs lightning fast and reached out to grab her shoulders, giving her a little shake before pulling her now shaking body against the hardness of his.

"I know. I was a bastard. A total and utter bastard. I can't ever ask or even expect you to forgive me for that.

It was inexcusable what I did—what I planned to do. But, Amira, I'm begging you, please give me—give us—another chance."

She pushed away from his hold. "Why should I? How can I trust you again? How do I know you don't have another strike against me up your sleeve?"

"I need you to trust me, like I should have trusted you. Please, can we talk about this downstairs?"

Amira gave a short nod and bent to pick up her mug before leading him back down the stairs and through to her apartment. She dropped into a chair and gave him a baleful stare. She still couldn't believe he was here. While her heart leapt in her chest, her mind still warned her to tread carefully.

"Go on then," she said flatly. "Talk."

Brent lowered himself onto the couch, his body dominating the piece of furniture.

"There's a lot I need to say to you, but before I start can you tell me why you broke off the wedding?"

"The wedding?" She looked startled. "You know why. Because of the proviso in Grandmother's will. I didn't know about it until it was too late—not that it mattered anyway."

"No. Not this wedding. The first one."

"What difference does it make? You weren't interested back then. Why now?"

"I came here straight from the church. Did you know that?"

Amira's expression told Brent she had no idea, confirming his belief that Isobel had orchestrated the whole thing as effectively as a military maneuver, including training her staff to head him off at the pass.

"Why?" She wasn't giving him an inch.

"To try and talk you back into going through with the wedding for one thing."

"If you were so keen to talk me into going through with the wedding, why didn't you try and contact me when we got back?"

"By then I was angry. At you, at Isobel. The whole damn world. When your housekeeper told me you and your grandmother had gone away, I wondered how long you'd been planning it. It all just seemed a little too slick for it to have been a spur of the moment thing. I was told you'd gone to the airport and that you wouldn't be back for a month or more. I ended up pouring all my frustration into work. By the time you got back, I was so busy trying to hold my business together that I wasn't prepared for anyone's excuses. It was wrong of me. But all I could focus on was protecting my name and my future." He rose and paced the carpet. "I'm not saying it was right. If anything it was probably a totally immature reaction. But that's done now. I can't turn back time, but I do concede I handled the whole situation very badly."

"Why didn't you tell me about the business?"

He stopped pacing and shoved his hands in his pockets. "At the time, I didn't want to worry you. Looking back now, I probably was feeling too insecure to want you to know—to give you an excuse to back out. Your grandmother had made it clear often enough that she didn't approve of me, that my financial position was no more than a drop in the bucket as far as she was concerned. I knew if she found out what was happening with my business before the wedding there was no way she'd let us go ahead. I didn't want to take that risk." He sat down in the chair opposite Amira, his forearms resting on his thighs as he leaned forward. "I didn't want to lose you, Amira, but I couldn't compete with her, could I?"

A flush stained Amira's throat, and her lower lip trembled. Damn, he hadn't meant to upset her again.

"She told me you'd deliberately withheld the information from me. From the moment I woke in the morning, she went on and on about it, waving the newspaper under my nose and telling me it wasn't too late. I was dressed in my gown, ready for the photographer. We were still arguing over it when she suddenly started to complain of chest pains. Our doctor came straight away and insisted she go to the hospital, but she refused to go unless I promised not to go ahead with the wedding.

"I had no choice, Brent. I was terrified I would kill her if I married you. I was incredibly hurt that you hadn't told me about what you were going through. I thought that if you kept that from me then what else were you hiding from me? That maybe Grandmother was right all along—that you only wanted to marry me because of my family's fortune and position in society. You were my first real boyfriend, my first love. We were about to be married. If I couldn't trust you, who could I trust? So I sent that text.

"After we went to the hospital, her tests came back

clear, and instead of coming home afterward, she'd arranged for our luggage to be brought to us and for a car to take us to the airport. She'd planned it all along. When I asked her about it, she told me she knew you'd let me down. Eventually I believed her."

Brent groaned. By trying to protect her, he'd ended up destroying them both.

"I had my reasons, my insecurities," he said quietly. "They were what drove me to succeed. I was too stupid to realize that I was driving you away at the same time." He thought back to his upbringing, to that sense of being beholden to his uncle for providing his education and then doing his utmost to pay him back. Of wanting never to have to rely on anyone for help in any shape or form. "How could I tell you my deepest fears? I didn't think you'd understand, coming as you did from a background of wealth."

"But that's what couples do. They support each other. Help one another. Stand together against their fears," Amira argued.

"I had to be able to give you what you already had, and more. How do you think I felt when I realized I was losing everything I'd worked so hard for. I couldn't lose you too."

"Money isn't everything. We would have managed."

"You say that when you've never wanted for anything. When you've never had to check a price tag or consider the cost of what you're wearing, what you drive, how you eat." Brent got up and paced again. "I felt I had to compete with all that, and when the papers blasted my news all over their pages that morning, I held on to the hope that you loved me enough to marry me anyway. I needed you more then than I'd ever needed you. And that's why I took the chance to have my revenge, to pay you back for choosing money over me."

Amira paled, her hands clenched into fists in her lap. Brent leaned forward and grasped her hands, slowly unpeeling her tightly knotted fingers and threading them through his own.

"Believe me. I am deeply sorry for what I put you through. Back then and now. I should have known Isobel wouldn't have given you a choice."

"I should have stood up to her," Amira whispered.

"How could you when she'd been manipulating you for so many years? She's gone now. She has no hold over you any longer."

Amira laughed—a raw sound that struck straight to his heart. "No hold over me? You know exactly what kind of hold she has over me. You've read her will. Even in death she's still trying to force me into motherhood or marriage, but not with the man I love. I honestly admit I used you to have a baby, but it was because I couldn't bear to think about marrying anyone else."

Brent latched on to the words he'd been hoping against hope to hear. *The man I love.*

"So if you couldn't marry anyone else, Amira, would you still marry me?"

"Don't!" She pulled her hands from his grasp and covered her face, her shoulders shaking as a sob racked her body.

"You said Isobel was trying to force you into marriage to someone you don't love. But if you could, would you marry me?" he pressed, determined to hear her answer.

"Yes."

He barely heard her through her tears. His heart twisted because he was once again causing her so much grief; but her answer sent a positive punch of hope through his body. She loved him. The knowledge suddenly made him feel ten feet tall and invincible. This was what he'd missed in his life. This was what had made that weekend at Windsong so special in those moments when he'd forgotten his vendetta against her.

And he knew without doubt he loved her too. Now all he had to do was convince her of it.

"Amira, look at me."

He reached out and took her hands, tearing them off her tear-streaked face.

"We can't let her win. Not now. Not when we still have the rest of our lives to be together. I love you too much to let you go again." He felt her stiffen at his words. Undeterred, he pressed on. "I was so wrapped up in paying you back for what had happened eight years ago that when I figured out you must be pregnant I had to see you. Had to see for myself that you'd hidden our baby from me. On top of everything else, it was the ultimate betrayal. I'll freely admit all I wanted to do at that stage was rip everything from your grasp.

"I already knew about the Fulfillment Foundation, and I'd set plans in motion to see you removed from the administration."

At Amira's shocked gasp he squeezed her hands firmly in his, drawing them to his lips and pressing a kiss to each.

"That was you? You took that from me too?" She wrenched free of his hold and rose on shaking legs.

He tried to stop her but she moved out of his reach, looking at him with eyes full of pain and accusation.

"I was a man bent on revenge. I had no thought for what it would do to you aside from take from you something personally important. To make sure you knew loss on every level the way I'd known it when you left me. In the past few years, whenever I've seen you featured in the papers or on TV, you've always been a figurehead, and I thought that was as deep as you went. Taking the foundation from you would have been nothing, especially when I saw the financial difficulty it was in. I arranged to make a sizable donation. But the donation was on the condition of you stepping down from your position there."

"How could you do that to me? It was all I had left." She turned her back on him. "Get out. Please just get out, and leave me alone."

"No! I've learned what a total idiot I was. I've seen that you're more than just a face on these charities you work for. They're a part of you as much as you're a part of them and their success. I couldn't take that from you now. I'm ashamed I ever dreamed I'd do that in the first place."

He stood up, staring at her back, his arms helpless at his side. He wanted nothing more right now than to drag her into his arms and try and comfort her for the hell he'd put her through—to make up for the pain he'd caused. But he had so much more to say to her first. To convince her they belonged together.

"Believe me, Amira. This past week I've learned a great deal about myself. Most of it I don't like. But one thing I have learned is how much you mean to me. How much I love you.

"When you collapsed on the island, I'd never been more scared or felt more helpless in my entire life. It was a wake-up call I hope never to get again. I thought I was going to lose you. One minute we were arguing and the next you were unconscious and bleeding. I would have given all my wealth and my right arm to know you were okay. I went with you to the hospital, but they separated us at emergency."

"I don't remember any of that. The first thing I remember was waking up in a recovery room and the doctor telling me—" Her voice broke off, and she shoved a fisted hand against her mouth.

A piece of Brent's heart tore away at the gesture, at the helplessness in her voice. He lifted his hands to take her into his arms to try to comfort her; but her body was stiff and unyielding in his embrace.

"Please, Amira. Don't reject me now. I tried to see you at the hospital. I waited, day after day, but they wouldn't let me near you. I had to see you. To tell you what a fool I'd been. To tell you how much I love you and how sorry I was for everything. Especially for the loss of our baby."

"But don't you see," Amira cried out, "it wouldn't matter. None of it matters anymore. I have nothing left. You've stripped me of every last thing that was mine."

"My solicitor told me this afternoon that you'd returned the foundation proposal letter, signed. I told him to tear it up. That the foundation was nothing without you. And I've instructed my accountant to return the money that you paid out to me. Your solicitor should have it in his trust account as we speak. I could never have kept it. Not even if our baby had lived. Let me make up my misjudgment to you. Let me love you as you deserve to be loved. Please, Amira, give me one more chance."

"I don't know if I can do that again, if I can trust you again."

"Do you love me?"

"What does that have to do with anything? I've always loved you, even when you've hurt me. What kind of pathetic person does that make me?"

"The kind of person who deserves the best of everything. The kind of woman I want to spend the rest of my life with. Marry me, Amira. Let the past go. Let Isobel and her ridiculous dictates go. Please, if you can find it in your heart to forgive me I promise you I will make it worth your while."

A crazed laugh shuddered through her as he repeated to her the words she'd uttered to him a few short months ago.

"I don't want you to make it worth my while."

Brent dropped his arms, let her go, his heart pounding. He'd lost her. Forever. The pain was indescribable. He stepped away from her, every cell in his body screaming at him not to.

"I'm sorry. You'll never know how sorry." He slowly walked toward the door. "I won't bother you again."

"Brent, stop." She ran across the room and threw her arms around him. "I said I don't want you to make it worth my while, but I never said I didn't want you to love me for all my life. We can't change what we've done to each other. But it's more than enough to me to be the woman you love. I love you. I'll always love you—every day and every night for the rest of my life."

"Will you marry me even though it'll mean saying goodbye to all of this?"

He swept an arm to encompass the home she'd lived in for eighteen years, and Amira suddenly understood that the bricks and mortar meant nothing to her now. Yes, it had been where she'd grown up. Yes, she was the last of the Forsythe line. And that was where it all ended. With her. Right now.

"Yes."

She looked around her. Aside from her father's portrait in the main house, there was nothing here she wanted to keep, nothing that was intrinsically hers. Nothing but the man in her arms.

"It doesn't matter anymore. Let Roland have it. Let him have it all. As long as I have you, I don't need anything else."

"I will look after you, you know—you and the family we're going to build together. And if you want, we can make Roland an offer he can't refuse for the place. Gerald Stein told me about your plans—how you wanted to turn it into a respite center and head office for the foundation. We can still do that. I'll make it happen if that's what you want."

Amira lifted her hand to stroke his face, the face that was so dear to her. She lifted her lips to his and kissed him, trying to imbue into her caress how much she meant what she'd just said. And he understood. She felt it in his body, in his kiss, in the way he held her.

"I want you," she said gently.

"Let's go home, then."

Brent took her by the hand and led her to his waiting car. As they walked out into the night, Amira realized the sensation of joy and lightness that suffused her was freedom. Freedom from Isobel's expectations, freedom from doing what had always been expected of her by others.

Freedom to love the only man she'd ever wanted.

* * * * *

Don't miss the second book in ROGUE DIAMONDS, *SECRET BABY, PUBLIC AFFAIR* *available March 2009* *from Silhouette Desire.*

Harlequin is 60 years old,
and Harlequin Blaze is celebrating!
After all, a lot can happen in 60 years,
or 60 minutes…or 60 seconds!
Find out what's going down in
Blaze's heart-stopping new mini-series,
FROM 0 TO 60!
Getting from "Hello" to "How was it?"
can happen fast….

Here's a sneak peek of the first book,
A LONG, HARD RIDE
by Alison Kent
Available March 2009

"Is that for me?" Trey asked.

Cardin Worth cocked her head to the side and considered how much better the day already seemed. "Good morning to you, too."

When she didn't hold out the second cup of coffee for him to take, he came closer. She sipped from her heavy white mug, hiding her grin and her giddy rush of nerves behind it.

But when he stopped in front of her, she made the mistake of lowering her gaze from his face to the exposed strip of his chest. It was either give him his cup of coffee or bury her nose against him and breathe in. She remembered so clearly how he smelled. How he tasted.

She gave him his coffee.

After taking a quick gulp, he smiled and said, "Good morning, Cardin. I hope the floor wasn't too hard for you."

The hardness of the floor hadn't been the problem. She shook her head. "Are you kidding? I slept like a baby, swaddled in my sleeping bag."

"In my sleeping bag, you mean."

If he wanted to get technical, yeah. "Thanks for the loaner. It made sleeping on the floor almost bearable."

As had the warmth of his spooned body, she thought, then quickly changed the subject. "I saw you have a loaf of bread and some eggs. Would you like me to cook breakfast?"

He lowered his coffee mug slowly, his gaze as warm as the sun on her shoulders, as the ceramic heating her hands. "I didn't bring you out here to wait on me."

"You didn't bring me out here at all. I volunteered to come."

"To help me get ready for the race. Not to serve me."

"It's just breakfast, Trey. And coffee." Even if last night it had been more. Even if the way he was looking at her made her want to climb back into that sleeping bag. "I work much better when my stomach's not growling. I thought it might be the same for you."

"It is, but I'll cook. You made the coffee."

"That's because I can't work at all without caffeine."

"If I'd known that, I would've put on a pot as soon I got up."

"What time *did* you get up?" Judging by the sun's position, she swore it couldn't be any later than seven now. And, yeah, they'd agreed to start working at six.

"Maybe four?" he guessed, giving her a lazy smile.

"But it was almost two…" She let the sentence dangle, finishing the thought privately. She was quite sure he knew exactly what time they'd finally fallen asleep after he'd made love to her.

The question facing her now was where did this relationship—if you could even call it *that*—go from here?

* * * * *

*Cardin and Trey are about to find out
that great sex is only the beginning….
Don't miss the fireworks!
Get ready for
A LONG, HARD RIDE
by Alison Kent
Available March 2009,
wherever Blaze books are sold.*

CELEBRATE
60 YEARS
OF PURE READING PLEASURE
WITH HARLEQUIN®!

**We'll be spotlighting a different series
every month throughout 2009
to celebrate our 60th anniversary.**

Look for Harlequin® Blaze™ in March!

0-60

*After all, a lot can happen in 60 years,
or 60 minutes...or 60 seconds!*

Find out what's going down in Blaze's
heart-stopping new miniseries *0-60!*
Getting from "Hello" to "How was it?"
can happen fast....

*Look for the brand-new **0-60** miniseries in March 2009!*

www.eHarlequin.com   HBRIDE09

REQUEST YOUR FREE BOOKS!

2 FREE NOVELS PLUS 2 FREE GIFTS!

Passionate, Powerful, Provocative!

You're invited to join our Tell Harlequin Reader Panel!

By joining our new reader panel you will:

- Receive Harlequin® books—they are FREE and yours to keep with no obligation to purchase anything!
- Participate in fun online surveys
- Exchange opinions and ideas with women just like you
- Have a say in our new book ideas and help us publish the best in women's fiction

In addition, you will have a chance to win great prizes and receive special gifts!
See Web site for details. Some conditions apply.
Space is limited.

To join, visit us at
www.TellHarlequin.com.

COMING NEXT MONTH
Available March 10, 2009

#1927 THE MORETTI HEIR—Katherine Garbera
Man of the Month
The one woman who can break his family's curse proposes a contract: she'll have his baby, but love must *not* be part of the bargain.

#1928 TALL, DARK...WESTMORELAND!—
Brenda Jackson
The Westmorelands
Surprised when he discovers his secret lover's true identity, this Westmoreland will stop at nothing to get her back into his bed!

#1929 TRANSFORMED INTO THE FRENCHMAN'S MISTRESS—Barbara Dunlop
The Hudsons of Beverly Hills
She needs a favor, and he's determined to use that to his advantage. He'll give her what she wants *if* she agrees to his request and stays under his roof.

#1930 SECRET BABY, PUBLIC AFFAIR—Yvonne Lindsay
Rogue Diamonds
Their affair was front-page news, yet her pregnancy was still top secret. When he's called home to Tuscany and demands she join him, will passion turn to love?

#1931 IN THE ARGENTINE'S BED—Jennifer Lewis
The Hardcastle Progeny
He'll give her his DNA in exchange for a night in his bed. But even the simplest plans can lead to the biggest surprises....

#1932 FRIDAY NIGHT MISTRESS—Jan Colley
Publicly they were fierce enemies, yet in private, their steamy affair was all that he craved. Could their relationship evolve into something beyond their Friday night trysts?

SDCNMBPA0209